VAIBHAV NEELA

CAPTAIN CATASTROPHE'S GREAT CATASTROPHE!

THE CRYSTALS OF RAILUX

First edition

Book formatting by Balasubramanian Nambi
Book cover designed by Nirkri (Fiverr)

Dedicated to my family and friends

About the Author:

Hi, my name is Vaibhav Neela and I am 14 years old. I am the author of 'Captain Catastrophe's Great Catastrophe!'

The idea for this book was generated through a creative writing competition(2019) where participants had to write a short story and submit it to an author who would judge the stories. I was chosen as a finalist for my story about two months later and ever since that moment I have always been thinking about the stories I write in my spare time.

Then a year later(2020), the COVID-19 pandemic hit the UK. This forced the country to go into lockdown and immediately, people were looking for things to do such as projects, hobbies and other activities. I came by the short story which I wrote in 2019 and I decided to continue it. I continued to write it for about two months where I had written the majority of the story.

I completed and published my book in mid 2021 with the great support from my family and friends. The creation of this book wouldn't have been possible without the loving support and thorough feedback from family, friends and others.

I'm very grateful to the reader who picked up this book and I very much hope you enjoy reading it.

Contents

....

CHAPTER 1

ACCIDENTS HAPPEN

He was one of the most cunning pirates of all time according to the stories and his legend had grown hugely. This was, of course, nowhere near the truth. When people spoke of him winning huge battles against inconceivable odds, it was nearly always an accident. He once tripped over a barrel, which allowed him to avoid a direct cannon ball shot to his body and sent a cannon ball directly into the weapons cache of another ship, blowing it to smithereens. A similar incident allowed him to defeat eight men when a rope he was nervously gripping tripped the men and sending most of them overboard.

His name was Captain Catastrophe. He had dreadlocked hair down to his shoulders, and a good-looking face. He had a slim but strong body. His hat, which was black and sewn with gold thread, was worn by his grandfather, Captain Calamity. He always tried to help people whenever he could. He liked to be on his ship which was called 'The Golden Fortune'.The ship was beautiful: it had tall, wooden masts that creaked in a fairly strong wind and large white sails that flapped and rustled in the wind. There were neatly organised barrels of salt fish, fruit, flour, water and rum on the decks. Next to them, also coils of thick braided rope. Slaves, carpenters and gunners were swarming the ship, their bare feet thumped against the cold wooden deck.

They were sailing across the Pacific Ocean and the sun was close to fading away. The horizon stretched across their entire field of view in the most amazing fashion. A massive expanse of crystal like water was all they could see ahead of them. The breeze caressed their skin, cooling them while the sun faded. Beautiful colours of orange and pink filled the dark blue sky and coloured the puffy white clouds. The calm ocean reflected the ship perfectly. The smell which the waves conjured was not fishy and disgusting as it was sometimes but rather a little salty.

Suddenly a great loud 'BOOM!!' had taken place at the bottom of the ship. Captain Catastrophe looked through his telescope from the ship's lookout and found a black flag with a red skull and crossbones in the middle, he then zoomed out of the strange image and soon found out that it was the ship called 'Scourge of Satan'. This ship's captain was Captain Dreadnaught. He had a reputation for looting, killing people and destroying ships. Captain Catastrophe immediately ordered his men to get their guns and cutlasses ready and especially the canons. Soon the beautiful scenery got destroyed by the wisps of silver grey smoke that curled and danced their way through the air and the yelling and thuds of people running on the deck.

As the enemy ship was getting closer, a second canon was fired: this time it was from Captain Catastrophe's ship. It shot across the water and created a small trail behind it and hit the ship straight into the deck. Splinters and large pieces of wood scattered in all directions; some people got blown away by the huge impact and fell into the watery depths below. Then, when the enemy ship was close to theirs, the swordsmen swung onto the ship and set wooden planks between the ships so that they could get across easily. There were loud yells and screams. There were deafening shots and explosions. Dark, maroon shades of red were everywhere on the wooden floored ships.

Captain Catastrophe was surrounded by Dreadnaught's men with razor-sharp cutlasses. He climbed up one of the masts and tried to keep distance between them. He then heard strange sawing noises. He looked down and soon found out: they were sawing the mast. Captain Catastrophe noticed a sail a few metres away from him. To his shock, the mast leaned forward with speed and he lunged towards the sail. The mast then fell on the men with a horrible crunch. And hanging on to a very high sail, was Captain Catastrophe.

CHAPTER 2

HIDDEN TALENTS

Captain Catastrophe lowered himself down and landed on the deck of the ship. Suddenly a bullet whizzed past him nearly obliterating his nose. It was Dreadnaught holding a gun. Captain Catastrophe went for his legs and knocked Dreadnaught off his feet. Soon Dreadnaught got up and threw a piece of wood at him which caused some bleeding, suddenly he had Catastrophe in a headlock. Then a shot was heard. Strangely, Dreadnaught was loosening his grip on him, then a thump as he hit the deck floor with a hole in his back. Then Catastrophe saw a woman who had a gun in her hand. She then walked over to Dreadnaught's body and looked at him menacingly and said, "That's for my uncle", and walked away.

It only seemed moments later but Captain Catastrophe woke up in a room. It looked like he fell unconscious due to the shortage of air in his windpipe when Dreadnaught put him in a headlock. He got up from the bed and found a door leading outside, "Good, at least the inside of the Golden Fortune is safe but I don't remember that door being there…"

He walked outside and found out that he was in a city, not the Golden Fortune. But that was not the only thing.

5 people with daggers creeped out of the alleyways and soon noticed Catastrophe. Catastrophe made a lot of foes along his journeys so this wasn't a rare occurrence. The only problem was that he had no weapons on him at that moment.

There was only one thing to do.

RUN.

Captain Catastrophe had all his weapons stripped off him when he was sleeping so he couldn't really fight the armed men. It looked like he was approaching a street market with all sorts of foreign items like pleasant smells of spices like cinnamon and the beauty of the ivory models. Catastrophe saw a necklace seller and snatched some bead necklaces, he then smashed it hard on the floor which made the beads come loose and were all over the floor. Clearly, the man selling the necklaces was furious and shouted curses at Captain Catastrophe. However, as the men were closing in on him, the slowest one didn't notice the beads on the floor unlike the others who couldn't be fooled easily and fell forward as his feet was on some beads causing him to slip with a yell.

There were now four men left chasing after Captain Catastrophe who had another idea, he grabbed a handful of salt and the fastest man behind Captain Catastrophe was catching up to him, nearly touching him so Catastrophe threw the salt in the man's face causing him scream quite loud and girlishly toppling towards the ground with an "OOF!!", three men were left and one of them said, "Take his left and you, take his right!" This was going to be a tricky situation to get out of. Then Captain Catastrophe found a horse with a saddle on and got on. The horse, who didn't seem to like other visitors on his back kicked off and went as fast as lightning. The three men could hardly be seen as they were so far away. Captain Catastrophe celebrated, "HA HA HA!!!", suddenly the horse stopped with such force Catastrophe flew off the horse's back and fell on the soft but prickly hay that was below him.

He found out that he was in a farm, and a huge one at that too. There was at least 80 acres of potatoes, corn and wheat and there were maybe a thousand animals there too. As Catastrophe looked around he saw a woman milking some cows and she looked like the exact woman who killed Dreadnaught. Catastrophe made a move towards her silently as he didn't want to startle her. Unfortunately for Captain Catastrophe, he didn't notice the twig under him.

SNAP!!

The woman turned around faster than Captain Catastrophe could say, "DAMN IT!", and she took her pistol out from her pocket and aimed at Catastrophe but when she noticed Catastrophe's face she put her gun down and said, "It's you again, did my people treat you well?"

"Yes I think they did but where am I and who are you?"

"My name is Jessica Tyger but you can call me Jess, and we are in the Kingdom of Railux."

"Well Jess, 5 men were trying to kill me out there and I had to get on a horse to escape them, I stopped 2 but I think 3 are coming this way right now!"

"Well if they are coming this way then they are running towards an unfortunate ending."

The 3 men soon got to the farm and said, “There he is! Get him.” Captain Catastrophe took a flintlock tucked under his coat and aimed at the men but then slipped on some cow-pat causing some of it to go flying into one of the men’s faces leading to him frantically shooting his pistol everywhere not noticing that his colleagues were in full range of the gun soon being torn to pieces by him until it ran out of bullets. Then Jess, whose blonde hair was all Catastrophe could see of her in the bright afternoon sun, shot the man’s back, probably killing him as Catastrophe heard a nail-biting crack of the man’s back.

“You are good at fighting, where did you learn all this?”, Jess asked, although Captain Catastrophe didn’t know if she was being sarcastic or not.

“Well, I learnt this from my mother, who was the one of the greatest warriors in the world.”

Jess then said, “I used to get trained by my mother; Antiope but she…has passed on.”Captain Catastrophe didn’t need to know what she was talking about. Antiope was dead.

“That’s the same thing with me, my mother died in war, but I’m glad she didn’t die in vain.”

Then Jess said,”We have quite a lot in common don’t we?”

“Yes, I guess so.”

“Oh, you should come over to the castle to be welcomed by my father, the king!”

It only took a moment for Captain Catastrophe to notice the gigantic castle on the tall hill behind the massive farm. Jess then whistled and a horse carriage came through the gateway and said, "Take me to the castle."

The man who was in the carriage nodded and opened the door to let Jess in but held out a hand, blocking Catastrophe and asked him, "Who are you?"

Jess said, "Gerald don't worry about him, he is my friend."

Gerald then let Catastrophe in and said, "My apologies sir, just doing my job."

Catastrophe said, "No problem."

Then the carriage left the farm and was going up the hill. The scenery was beautiful; there were so many green trees that it looked like there was a massive green blanket. Then when they arrived at the castle it looked 10 times bigger than it looked like from the farm. Captain Catastrophe then asked Jess, "If you're so rich and powerful how come you were milking cows?"

Jess then said, "Just because I am the Princess of Railux doesn't mean I leave my daily duties."

They then entered through the main castle gate and there were guards everywhere. Jess then led Catastrophe to the main hall where her father was. The hall had huge quartz pillars chiseled with pictures of weapons and warriors. The chandeliers were beautifully made with polished and cut glass. The fountains drizzled on the rough rocks and the flowers growing nearby had a sweet honey smell. Caught in all of this beauty, he didn't realise the King was right in front of him(at the end of the hall) so Catastrophe said, "Greetings, your Majesty."

The King replied, "Captain Catastrophe! One of the world's most famous pirates! So good to meet you. It seemed that you helped my daughter in the battle against Alexander Dreadnaught so I would like to reward you with something",He called one of his servants who was holding a bag of money to give it to Captain Catastrophe.

Catastrophe responded, "Thank you so much your Majesty, It is also of great honour that I am speaking to you."

"To prove your strength and power I am providing a challenge which you and my daughter will succeed in."

"So what exactly am I doing this for, your Majesty?"

"As we speak, a curse is upon this world and when the countdown ends the whole world will be ended with disasters, monsters and diseases."

Catastrophe looked at Jessica. Jessica looked at Catastrophe.

Catastrophe then said, "Alright your Majesty, what do you want me to do?"

"I need you to retrieve the five crystals of Railux. From all we know, they were all part of one crystal that was destroyed aeons ago. The 5 crystals are each guarded by some sort of creature. When the crystals are put together it will end the curse. Your strength, your intelligence and your adaptability will prove worthy in this quest."

"I also have a map that has four crystals pointed on it but the last one is not there. When you find the four crystals they should guide you on the map to the last crystal."

Captain Catastrophe looked at the map and found the nearest crystal and he and Jessica set off to Chailium where the first crystal was kept. Despite knowing the general location of the crystal, they didn't know the exact location of the crystal, let alone what it was being guarded by. Anyways, with optimistic hearts, they got on two white horses and rode to Chailium. According to the map, it was around 120 miles away from Railux. As they were riding they were having a conversation;

"So, do you have any other surprises, Catastrophe?"asked an annoyed Jess, who would quite frankly want to do this mission herself. She didn't need help from an amateur.

"Well, I'm good at painting," said Catastrophe

"Painting huh? You could teach me a few tricks."

"Yeah, I guess so."

CHAPTER 3

THE HUNT BEGINS

They arrived at Chailium, the smallest kingdom in the region but it was also one of the most feared as it is said they keep monsters to torture their victims. This sparked an idea in Captain Catastrophe's head;

"Hey, if this place is infested with monsters, the thing guarding the crystal must be a monster of some sort."

"But there's no point in knowing what's guarding it if we don't know exactly where the crystal is!" Said Jess

"That is true, but where do we start?"

"Let's ask some people, they might know where the crystal is being kept."

A man, having heard this conversation, waddled towards them and spooked Catastrophe. Catastrophe could have sworn he saw a smirk from the corner of his eyes from Jess but ignored it.

"Sir, who are you?" Asked Catastrophe.

"My name is Jeffrey Wilson and I am a wandering trader which if you didn't know what a wandering trader is, he/she is a person who travels around the world, trading foreign items for money and then repeating the same process again and again!"

"Do you know anything about a crystal of Railux in this area?"

Ah, well, you see, I do this trading business for a cost and I can tell you a lot more than you think I know about the crystal of Fire."

"Jeffrey, I'm sorry if I misheard you but did you just say the crystal of Fire?" inquired Jess.

"Yes, the crystal of Fire is one of the five crystals of Railux. There are also the crystals of Water, Air and Earth but no one knows what the Fifth one is."

"Hmmm, 10 silvers for the information." Said Jess, and handed over 10 silver coins.

"That is a good deal."

"Ok then Jeffrey, what do you know?"

"Only a few know about the crystal of Fire. It's kept in the north tower of the castle and it's guarded by a creature called Morphon; a creature that can replicate your abilities and use them against you but in a more methodical and smarter way. But I believe it has a weakness." Catastrophe and Jess listened carefully.

"The way Morphon copies other people's abilities is by this sort of glowing rope with a 3-legged plunger on the end. It attaches to its enemy and takes its best weapons to replicate and destroy. As the rope is exposed, someone could easily cut it off and it would just become a creature as harmless as a baboon."

Suddenly an arrow was shot that narrowly missed Catastrophe's head but did hit Jeffrey straight through his head. He then flopped to the floor, still. Jess took her pistol out and shouted, "Who's there!?"

Then, a head popped out of the bushes holding a crossbow but in a few seconds wasn't anymore as there was a shot from Jessica's gun straight in the head. Then another man appeared behind a tree which was just in front of them but Jess then took her knife and ran at the man. Catastrophe saw a man with a vicious look on his face with a crossbow who aimed at him and shot the arrow.

However, Catastrophe slipped on the leaves below him causing the arrow to miss and miraculously hit the man who Jess was fighting in the back. Captain Catastrophe then said to the man who just shot his own partner in the back, "Not having a good day are you?," and then punched him in the face causing him to fall unconscious. "That was some skill Catastrophe," said Jessica with an impressive smile on her face.

CHAPTER 4

THE CRYSTAL OF FIRE

"Anyways, who were those guys?" said Jess

"Probably thieves or bandits," said Catastrophe.

"We have to get to the North Tower as stealthily as possible or we'll get caught!"

"That's it! We have to get caught in order to fight Morphon!" exclaimed Catastrophe.

"What!?"

"Remember how Jeffrey said that you could get a one-way ticket to Morphon if you got caught for committing a terrible crime? Well if we could commit a crime, we could hopefully get sent to Morphon and kill him on the spot!"

"Or we could just go into an arena and fight him there." Jess pointed at a sign that said, 'Beat the unstoppable creature; Morphon and win whatever you desire(no one as of yet has won).'

"Oh, we might as well enter ourselves into it." The sign said 'come to the main entrance to sign up and depending on the queue(which will be a very short one) you will be treated to quickly.'

They walked over to the castle gate and spoke to the guard and said, "We are here to fight Morphon!"

The guard let out a laugh and said, "Another casualty that I won't be speaking to ever again" and let them in. Captain Catastrophe then was thinking "He's not serious, right?" and walked down with Jess to the main hall where the king was sitting at the end of the hall. This castle's main hall was horrendous compared to Railux Castle. Shards of broken glass covered the floor and blood stained the carpet.

"Yes, yes I know it is not the cleanest castle in the world but it will do for now. So you are the 12th and 13th people to enter this castle to challenge my most powerful, bloodthirsty, nerve-racking monster, and you are not showing a single bit of fear."

"We have come here for the crystal of Fire."

"How do you know that?"

"We found out from a wandering trader. He's dead now."

"Well, it won't matter anyway because you are going against..." he paused for a second and then a blood-curdling scream was let out and then a squelch and finally an inhuman roar.

"If you beat Morphon, You will get the crystal of Fire."

"Alright then, bring it on!", said Jess in a brave tone. Captain Catastrophe then looked at the king and stared into his eyes with quite seriousness as the king was too. The king then said, "Prepare for the next battle." A man to the right of Captain Catastrophe then gripped Jessica's arm and said, "Come with me you beauty," then Jess took her knife and cut a deep cut in the man's arm. "Don't try that," said Jess.

The king then said, "She's got guts."

Then another man came to help take Catastrophe and Jess to a gate which was leading to a whole section of the castle. The large gate opened and two men pushed them inside, then suddenly the gate closed with a bang. There was a little cave where an arm popped out and gestured 'follow me'. Jess and Catastrophe then followed with their weapons out: a sword and Captain Catastrophe's Golden Flintlock. Jess said, "Stop! It's a trap!" Captain Catastrophe then looked at the tripwire so thin and incredibly hard to notice. "How did you notice that?" enquired Catastrophe.

"I noticed the huge metal blades in the slits of the walls." And she was right; humongous blades of metal that looked like it could chop an elephant in two pieces. They proceeded towards another path which had a lit archway and a engraved sign that said "follow the light."

"I guess we follow the torches," said Catastrophe.

"Yes," said Jess. They followed the torches that lit up the path until they were presented with 3 doors that were made out of stone with creepers and moss crawling along the door like a hideous green spider. Then a whispering voice that sounded like a gurgling human spoke:

"So you are not the average fatality that I fight are you? Well, in front of you, you see three doors, the door first to the left has a young basilisk which if I told you what it was, you'd probably kill yourself before it had the chance to rip you to pieces. The door first to the right has a room infested with cobras, and the door in the middle has two lions who haven't eaten in 4 weeks. I could be lying, but it's up to you to figure it out." The unusual voice stopped.

Then it spoke again, "Oh did I forget to mention that you have approximately half a minute to choose a door or poison-tipped arrows will shoot through the holes in the wall. If you are wondering if I am bluffing or not, allow me to give you a demonstration."

A man walked towards them. He had a bag over his face and was muttering prayers. It seemed that he was a prisoner of some sort.

Then the gurgling voice spoke again, "This man's name is William Cundelburry. He was one of our most loyal soldiers but had fallen for some girl in another kingdom and gave our plans away for a future battle we were going to have with them. Any last words William?"

The man was silent for a short time and then said, "Follow the light." An arrow suddenly shot through his back and then the man started writhing in agony all over the floor and was screaming horrifyingly, "KILL ME!, JUST END IT!!" and fell, his body motionless.

"Your time starts now."

CHAPTER 5

FOLLOW THE LIGHT

Jess was looking at the torches. Catastrophe was looking at the same torch as well. "We've got to go for the door in the middle," said Jess, "It's the only door with a torch above it meaning that we follow the light!" Catastrophe knew there was no other option but to trust Jess on this and it also seemed the most logical choice. The engraved sign that said 'follow the light' and William's last words must have meant something. Catastrophe knew that there was no way a lion could live for four weeks without food, let alone hunt for food. "Yes, we have to."

They went for the door and opened it. After a few moments, they could hear the high pitched thumping of arrows against the door when they closed it. That was a close call. There were two lions, both sleeping or dead. But they couldn't take any chances so they walked very quietly to another door that seemed to be only a hundred yards away but from there it felt like a mile. Soon they realised it wasn't only two lions but 20, all sleeping or dead. Then, they heard a growling sound from behind them;

"Catastrophe?" said Jess anxiously.

"Run!" shouted Catastrophe. They ran as fast as they could to the door but the worst thing that happened, happened. The door was locked and all the lions were charging towards them. There was about only 10 seconds before they were eaten alive. Then, the most abnormal thing happened; a lion who was clearly the fastest of the lot, was nearing Jess and Catastrophe. It then leaped at Catastrophe whose back was against the door. But then Catastrophe slipped on the wet floor below him and fell flat as the lion was heading for the wooden door and crashed into it, causing enough shock for the door to open and leaving the lion with a pretty bad headache.

Jess helped Catastrophe up and ran through the doorframe. "Close the door!" yelled Jess as the small battalion of lions were heading towards them both. Catastrophe closed the door, with a series of bangs on the door immediately after. Catastrophe stuck his dagger in a gap between the door and the floor, locking the door temporarily.

"Well, that was hard work, wasn't it?" said Jess who was sweating. Catastrophe handed her a water satchel.

"Where are we now then?" asked Jess. Then suddenly, torches were lighted and there was the gurgling voice again: "So you seek the crystal of Fire don't you? Well, You've gotten past one of my best traps and killed all those lions but there is one more challenge…"

Suddenly, a creature was revealed on the chandelier of the last room which was quite big like a miniature arena but ruined. It was a hideous monster with one of its arms(which had short crystallised purple spikes) stitched to its body, which was blue and yellow and its other arm was like a claw but it was wrapped in dragon skin. It's feet were yellow and had only two toes. And its face would give even the bravest and greatest knight nightmares. It didn't have a mouth, instead it had a long slit going down the middle of his face between his purple eyes which had teeth on it.

"I've been watching you ever since you entered my lair and now meet your end. I. AM. MORPHON!"

Morphon suddenly headed for Jess, Jess was waiting for the right moment to strike with her sword but Morphon knocked it down to the floor with his corrupted claw. His claw was about to strike again, but this time it was heading for Jess's head. Then Catastrophe took his flintlock out and shot Morphon through the side of his chest but then it looked like his chest just sucked the bullet in and repaired its skin. Morphon's chest opened up revealing a blue tube with a suction like plunger on the end of it that shot out at Captain Catastrophe who braced himself.

The suction rope hit him so hard it knocked him backwards. Then Captain Catastrophe noticed a torch next to him and yanked it out of its holder. He then jabbed the top of the torch into the suction rope causing it to return back to Morphon. Then, Morphon's arms transformed into massive battle axes and was screaming deafeningly. Morphon, who's attention was focused on Catastrophe, walked towards him, his steps making squelching noises. Jess, however took her sword and jumped on Morphon's back and plunged her sword through the deafening creature's head causing him to fall forward with a thump. Captain Catastrophe then ran at Morphon and then pulled his suction rope out and cut it with his cutlass. He was dead.

Suddenly, Morphon's body disintegrated into dust and then all that was left was a red crystal that was about half the size of Catastrophe's palm. Jess took it and examined it. "Wait is that what I think it is?"asked Captain Catastrophe.

"It's the crystal of Fire!" exclaimed Jess. She put the crystal in her pocket. "We need to get out." It looked like the walls of the arena were made out of 7 inch thick stone bricks. There was an option though. There was a window with wooden planks boarded against it and the window was big enough for both of them to go through. Catastrophe tried kicking the planks down but they were pretty strong. Jess then tried kicking the door down but then something unbelievable happened. Around Jess there were circling flames of fire that went around in a spiral sort of motion. "What's happening to me?!" exclaimed Jess. It did not hurt Jess but it did feel strange to her. "I'm alright but there's this strange sensation that I have an overload of energy, maybe I should kick the board again?" She kicked the board down again but this time the planks exploded in flames.

"Whoa!" yelled Jess. The wood had been obliterated. "This is not normal. Well we should figure out how I got thees -" She paused midway in her sentence as the fire streaks spiralling around her had stopped and it looked like they were going somewhere, it in fact went to the exact pocket that the fire crystal was kept in.

"Do you think the crystal gave you Fire abilities?" asked Catastrophe.

"Yes, it's the only reason possible. Also, it's called the Fire crystal for a reason."

"True."

"Well, let's get out of here. I don't think the king is going to be too happy about his monster."

"Agreed."

CHAPTER 6

AQUARION - THE UNDERWATER KINGDOM

"So, what's the next place on our map, Captain?" asked Jess.

"First of all, you don't have to call me *captain* and second of all, I think we should go to Aquarion because it's the closest to Chailium and it's a nice place."

"It's a nice place?"

"Well it is hidden behind one of the biggest waterfalls in the world."

"Alright then, let's go."

"Where are our horses?" asked Catastrophe.

"Oh…"

"I mean we could just take those ones over there, they have saddles on."

They rode to Aquarion and took some supplies with them in some markets like food, ammunition and water.

As the ride to Aquarion was quite long, this sparked some conversation between Catastrophe and Jess;

"So, Catastrophe, do you have any surprises left to show me?" asked Jess, who had doubts about Catastrophe from the beginning of the trip but started to trust him after seeing what he could do against Morphon.

"Maybe, I guess we'll have to wait and see." Said Catastrophe, who could tell that Jess was being slightly suspicious of his ability. The conversation was soon over and the journey to Aquarion was coming to an end.

They soon arrived at Aquarion which at first seemed to be a humongous waterfall.

"Come on, do we have to go through!?" said Captain Catastrophe, reluctantly.

"There is a entrance through those rocks over there."

There was a sort of arch to the right of the waterfall. They went through it and saw a busy town with fountains at every corner of it and an elegant and large castle surrounded by thatched roof houses which were also large and tempting to live in. It seemed there were no paths so they had to travel by boat to get around. So, Catastrophe and Jess met a man who seemed to have a boat up for sale. They brought a boat and started exploring the city. Then, they went into a place which had hundreds of guards. And the guards(one a man with a scar on his face and the other was a woman, who seemed to have no hair) asked them if they were newcomers;

"Yes, we just wanted to see this beautiful kingdom here", said Jess.

"As nice of a couple you are, we will have to search you."

"We're not together." Jess said repulsively, as the soldiers searched them. As the guard searched Jess, he felt the crystal in her pocket and took it out. "What's this?"

Jess, who panicked for a few seconds, responded, "Oh, sorry that's part of my rock collection."

"Huh, alright."

Jess thought to herself, '*Close call.*'

The soldiers then put their thumbs up to a soldier nearby and then said, "You're all good."

"Thank you, what are those?" Jess was pointing to the two strange leaves that another soldier had.

"Oh, these? Well you're going to need these leaves if you're going underwater to see the real castle of Aquarion."

"What exactly do you mean by the 'real castle'?" enquired Catastrophe

"Well, It is called the underwater kingdom for a reason!"

The soldier who had the leaves then gave both of them to Captain Catastrophe and Jess. He told both of them to eat them when you are about to enter the water as apparently they would give them the ability to breathe underwater and swim as fast as a dolphin. Captain Catastrophe then saw a pool that seemed to be for diving.

Jess and Catastrophe proceeded to the pool but as they did they felt a huge shock as the ground shook violently causing some people around them to fall. Then they heard a massive roar from underneath them.

"Jess, are you alright?" said Catastrophe, as Jess had fallen over due to the massive shock.

"That was a big one wasn't it lads?" said the soldier. Clearly, he knew that Jess and Catastrophe had no idea what he was talking about.

"That huge shock you just felt was not any earthquake and neither was that deafening sound you heard. That is Krolion, the giant monster as tall as our castle that is part kraken, part dragon but a human body shape. He's never been defeated in a battle before as anyone who's even took a glance at him will run or swim away scared! He rips ships apart like cotton and smashes mountains for fun."

"Does he live underwater?" Asked Jess.

"No in fact Krolion lives in a vast cave because of his human lungs he can't survive underwater for long. The cave is so large it once took a man one year to find his way back out. Anyways, the king had a deal with Krolion so it won't attack the castle. Have a nice day!" The soldier then left them alone.

"No, I am not fighting a mad kraken dragon man who is the size of this castle. I can deal with a corrupted monster who lives on killing people with traps but not this kind of threat!" exclaimed Catastrophe.

"Hey, calm down, you're forgetting that we have something on our side." She held up the crystal of Fire which was in her pocket the whole time. Well, that crystal did give Jess the ability to destroy things using fire. Maybe they stood a fighting chance. Then, suddenly a man ran across Jess and snatched the crystal out of her hand.

"Hey!" yelled Jess, as she was running after the man. The man then took a knife out and faced Jess with the knife glinting in the sunlight. Jess went for his legs but the man immediately reacted and took a slash at Jess's arm but instead of Jess screaming in pain, she knocked the man over. The man then got back up with his knife in his hand but the only problem was is that there was no blade. Instead there was a small pile of molten metal on the floor below him. Despite the shock the man had just received, he punched Jess in the side of her chest. Strangely she didn't react to the punch. But then the man was screaming because unbelievably his hand was on fire. Jess knew that the crystal must have had some effect on her and could use fire to fight other people. Then, the man dropped the crystal on the floor and ran as fast as he could from Jess.

Catastrophe arrived at the scene. He was in shock, but glad to get the Fire crystal back.

"That Fire crystal could actually help us defeat Krolion, don't you think?"

"Yeah, I think we should go back now."

"Alright then let's go."

They soon arrived at the diving area and got these underwater sort of suits that would help to cope with the temperature. Captain Catastrophe was quite scared as he had a phobia of being underwater. However, Jess was looking forward to it.

"Come on, it's not going to be that bad!" said Jess. Then some soldiers who were watching the diving area said, "It's your first time here right? Well in that case, just follow the others to the castle and you will be alright."

Catastrophe and Jess got in the water and then suddenly an incredibly strong current pulled them in, and it didn't seem to stop. Jess was holding her position as the current was getting stronger, however Captain Catastrophe was flailing about, clearly awful at swimming.

Then the current then slowed down a lot as they were being taken into the castle that actually two times the size of Chailium's castle. Then Captain Catastrophe heard the same ground-shaking roar of Krolion. Inside the castle were hundreds of blue shiny crystals and strange creatures that had never been seen before. There were some humanoid sort of creatures holding tridents. And that wasn't even the strangest thing. They had a squid head with tentacles. Suddenly, they moved towards Jess and Catastrophe and said, "The king is resting at the moment, you may have a look around the castle but however famous you are in the outside world, you are still treated as a guest to our kingdom."

Jess and Catastrophe looked around the castle and saw many bioluminescent creatures that had beautiful patterns on their skin. They then swam to what was apparently the garden.

You could call it a coral garden. The coral was dusky pink and orange with white tops, and on first glance was quite empty. Then a crab scuttled across a natural sand road. With pincers raised he made his side-ways scuttle across the sand and went into a little hole. Then Jess screamed as a humongous hand the size of Catastrophe's ship grabbed a nearby cliff and what Catastrophe saw next was staggering.

CHAPTER 7

KROLION

A shadow of a vaguely titan like outline emerged from the massive chasm below. It had an octopus-like head whose face was a mass of feelers, a scaly, rubbery-looking body, standing-out claws on it's hind and fore feet, and long, narrow wings behind. To Captain Catastrophe it resembled an octopus, a dragon and a human all in one, 100ft tall, with webbed human-looking slender arms and legs and a pair of dragon wings on its back. The monster's head was of a gigantic octopus, with many tentacles surrounding its mouth. Catastrophe immediately took Jess by her hand and swam back to the castle. Obviously, Catastrophe being an atrocious swimmer, the massive creature's head appeared just behind the coral garden, it's red glowing eyes shining. Then the massive creature spoke in a low voice that echoed through the whole castle, "Ah, new visitors I see, no need to be scared of me, I only eat people when I am told to, but lucky for you, it's not feeding time" He then returned back to the chasm. Then Catastrophe asked Jess if she was okay.

"Yes, but that was unbelievable. How are we supposed to beat that thing? And also what about the crystal of water?

Where's that hidden?" Jess said, nearly unable to breathe from shock.

"From our experience against Morphon, I think it probably gives him the powers of breathing underwater."

"That is possible but why didn't Morphon have any ability of using fire against us when we were fighting him?"

"He probably didn't want anyone to know he had such powers. I mean, lots of people know about the crystal of Fire, everyone in Railux knows, so it's possible that he wanted to hide those powers in case anyone was spying on him." Said Captain Catastrophe.

Then they heard a deafening sound like a massive horn from inside the castle. Could that mean something was going on?

"Maybe the king woke up?" suggested Captain Catastrophe, who was wondering what the strange noise was. Then a loud voice that was being projected said "the king has woken!" "Well then, let's go talk to him." Then they went through the castle doors and was then greeted by a hearty "Hello!" by an old man with a massive sceptre in his left hand and then said, "What brings you here to Aquarion?" Captain Catastrophe then said, "We mean no harm sir but who exactly are you apart from the King Of Aquarion?"

"Not a question I get asked usually, but my name is Marius Neptune. My name was given by the god of the sea Neptune himself. I was an ambitious person who loved the sea and studied them a lot."

"Who's 'them'? asked Jess, as she suddenly was intrigued by the old man's words.

"Mermaids and leviathans of the sea!" exclaimed the man.

"Well, mermaids I have seen, but leviathans! I've only seen krakens and giant squids but leviathans are humongous!" said Catastrophe.

"Ah Yes, I can command them all right here, right now, but we don't want to end Aquarion and the world today!"

"Oh," said Jess, who didn't really care about any other type of leviathans except one.

"Tell me about Krolion, I ne- I mean we need to know more about him."

The mood in the castle went dark. "Now listen to me very carefully," the guards suddenly lifted their spears "Krolion is more than a leviathan- he is a sentinel. Sentinels are leviathans that are much more powerful than the regular ones I just told you about. Each sentinel have different powers and come in different sizes and shapes. You thought the Minotaur was a creature who dwelled in a maze on land? No, he is a sentinel and dwelled in a maze in the sea. Krolion is one of the strongest sentinels out there currently and with the Water crystal he is nearly invincible. In fact, I should tell you why our beautiful kingdom is hiding this terrible secret.

CHAPTER 8

A SINKING KINGDOM

"BOOM!" A fiery ball of wood went straight through the North Tower, making the cone shaped dome crumble causing hundreds of bricks chipping the stairways. The woman took cover under a small porch, she had to get up to the top. It was time for the world to change. She reached the top of the tower and opened a secret door which looked like a wall and then a golden light shone through and a golden, jewel encrusted trident was lodged between a statue's hands.

Then, the woman spoke in an unusual language and then the trident fell out of the statue's hand and she took it and got out of the secret room. "This place is going to be a pile of rocks in a moment" She then spoke to the trident as it was a person and said, "Protect my son, I grant him the power of Aquarion!" The thunder seamed to crack the air, as if the black clouds might split apart. It rolled like the ash could of a volcano, becoming a rolling booming rumble.

Then the job was done, she had succeeded and the people of Aewaledora would have a better future. Then with the force of Zeus, lightning struck the opposing army and then a river burst its banks, destroying the catapults and hurling men around and killing them instantly with the force of thousands of gallons. She ran down the stairs as fast as she could to get back to her son and then take him to the dungeons where he and she would be safe. She was midway through the tower and gazed through the window to see hundreds of men and objects destroyed. What she just noticed however was a tiny glowing dot in the sky, it then got bigger and bigger and then… BOOM! Suddenly the whole tower exploded in a fiery inferno as two more fire balls hit the tower in the middle and the bottom. It was raining hot stones like meteors.

The king William Neptune stood still, unable to move as that was the tower that his wife was in and there was no point in searching for her as the explosion was fatal. He then rushed back to the castle to retrieve his son. He arrived at his son's room and took his son, fortunately he was safe but there was something strange about him; there were strange blue markings on his skin but they weren't scars, they looked like they were perfect cuts. Despite this strange occurrence, King Neptune took the boy and ran back outside.

A few years ago, his wife told him a story about an underwater kingdom called Aquarion which used to be a kingdom that was on ground but after a spell was cast, the ground opened up to a massive kingdom ten times the size of their current one. Then, the people who were falling through the massive ravines and cracks from the shockwave came to a slow motion movement; they were underwater. The source of the water came from these massive tunnels that were still releasing water out, at least a hundred thousand gallons a second. Strangely, that was exactly what was happening right now.

It was nearly impossible to imagine all of this happening at once, in fact they were so confused and shocked that they didn't know they were breathing underwater. King Neptune, who had been spun, tumbled and pushed around by the currents, managed to keep hold of his son, but his son was flashing blue and green like an aurora. He then came to a halt, and looked around him; there were hundreds of citizens and soldiers flailing about in the water, in total confusion about what was going on. Then he saw the gigantic castle below him. It looked like the materials used to make it were pure metal because it was very shiny. Distracted by the castle, he didn't see the massive hand grab a cliff about a few hundred metres away from him. Then, there was a boom and another which did catch his attention.

It was only then he noticed Krolion.

What King Neptune was staring at was what the legends had said; a monster which was 100ft tall, had massive wings on its back and red, glowing eyes that stared back into King Neptune's eyes. The massive creature spoke in a deep, ominous tone, "You must be King Neptune, my name is Krolion and I require something from you."

"The legends are true!?" exclaimed King Neptune, surprising himself as he could speak underwater as clearly as he could speak on land.

"Oh yes, they are very true indeed" said Krolion, "All I need from you is to give me your son for a short while and in return I will leave you alone and protect you from threats and make sure the people are safe."

"This is outrageous! Our castle has been destroyed, All of our people are scared and confused and you come out of nowhere asking for my last possession; my son!?"

"Well, when you put it like that, yes."

"Why do you need him anyway?"

"Your wife summoned the power of the water crystal and granted your son power of Aquarion. I have come here to extract it from him. I knew that you wouldn't take kindly to this idea but he will come to no harm and you will get him back in a short while."

"How can you possibly believe that I would trust you, of all people and creatures?"

"Just give him to me or else…" Krolion's vast hand started to move towards King Neptune and held him up to his face.

King Neptune was looking straight into Krolion's glowing red eyes.

"Okay, take him but please return him. If he comes to any harm, I will…"

"HaHAHA" the sentinel laughed, "Well what are you going to do? Fight me?"

The king was speechless and watched as the massive sentinel, who had his son, swam back into the cave in which it had appeared from.

CHAPTER 9

THE BATTLE OF AQUARION

"And I never saw him again." Said the king sadly. Captain Catastrophe and Jess were shocked after hearing the story.

"I've sent multiple troops to get my son back, but when they go in they never come back. Every time Krolion visits me, he warns me not to send anymore otherwise he will bring destruction to this kingdom and kill everyone here. I wish you could help but how would you? Have you faced any mythical monsters of any sort?"

"We've killed Morphon!" Exclaimed Captain Catastrophe.

"What? Morphon? Impossible, I don't believe it. Do you have any proof ?"

Jess was going to take out her Fire crystal but no one but only her and Catastrophe knew about Morphon's secret. They were going to have to tell King Neptune about it.

"This here," said Jess, "is the Fire crystal." She held it up so everyone could see it. "When we defeated Morphon, he disintegrated into dust and all that was left was this. This is the best proof we have."

"Actually, I think I might have accidentally put this in my rucksack," said Catastrophe. He took out the replicator from Morphon(the three-pronged plunger that could replicate weapons and abilities) and showed it to the King.

"Well, two amazing pieces of proof! So I assume you are great warriors from ancient civilisations?"

"No I'm from…well I don't really remember where I was from. My mother died giving birth to me and my father went somewhere and he never came back." Said Catastrophe.

"I'm from Railux." said Jessica.

"Okay, I am entrusting you to retrieve my son from Krolion's cave and if you can, end the monster. I will send my Aquarions with you. And just before you leave, take this armour. It was made by the old Aquarion kings and it can absorb massive forces of around 5000 tonnes. It is also made of extremely reflective material that when you hit the wristbands of your armour together they will spark and shine a blindingly bright light."

"Also take these tridents, they have five prongs and covered in poison that damages the victim's nervous system. It's made of an extremely lightweight but also very strong material. Now go, kill Krolion and bring my son back"

Captain Catastrophe had never been a leader of an army before. There were at least 5,000 soldiers who would act on his command.

BOOM! Something burst through the castle hallway, destroying the pillars and walls which crumbled and slammed into the ground. It was Krolion. He grabbed a nearby chunk of rock and threw it at some of the stunned soldiers, who soon got crushed. Soldiers threw their tridents at Krolion, which did little damage, but was enough to enrage him. His tentacle beard extended and grabbed the soldiers who didn't have tridents and constricted them like a snake would, and killed them. Jess threw her special trident and it hit Krolion's foot. He shouted in pain and then swam away, back into his cave.

Catastrophe, Jess and the soldiers who could walk checked on the injured soldiers and were sent to the healers where they would hopefully make a fast recovery. Krolion must have heard the plan to kill him. He couldn't kill all the soldiers as that would be a suicidal mission. He instead planned a hit and run attack so he could prepare for this war back at his cave. Catastrophe heard a grunting noise; "Someone must still be here." Catastrophe looked through the rubble and found the source of the sound coming from the end of the hallway. He ran to the pile of rubble and started digging. He found something that shocked him greatly; a crown. He called Jess and some Aquarion soldiers over and they frantically dug and dug until they found King Neptune. He was alive, but extremely weak. It was unlikely he was going to make it and he himself knew that too and said, "Go, gather the remaining soldiers and make your way to Krolion's cave. And just before you go, I need you to take this, it's a self destruct button, if you can't take down Krolion and he is too much for you, press it and the vortex bombs positioned all around the kingdom will destroy Aquarion in half an hour. Make sure you get our people to safety.Now go..."

The king was taken away to hopefully be healed by the healers but the damage may have been too much for the old man to handle. More soldiers were sent to bring the count of soldiers to 7,000.

It was time to take down Krolion.

Captain Catastrophe, Jess and the army of Aquarions were heading into Krolion's cave. Catastrophe told many soldiers to wait outside the cave, in case he escaped. Now they were in the cave and it was like any other cave but massive. As the army proceeded they heard strange noises coming from the cave. It had to be Krolion. Suddenly, the stalactites from the cave ceiling fell from a shockwave that Krolion roared. They still proceeded until they came to a halt because something moved near the cave walls. A creature sped towards Jess, who was its closest target. A mutated octopus-shark attacked Jess as quick as lightning. Catastrophe aimed his trident at the octoshark and threw it but missed pathetically as it hit a stalactite. However the stalactite was dislodged from the cave ceiling and it's sharp point on the end of it penetrated the octoshark's body as it was pulled down from the immense weight of the stalactite.

"Another accident to add to the list' Said Catastrophe, "are you okay?"

"Yes, I'm fine, Krolion probably has more of those coming our way."

As Catastrophe wrenched his trident out of the rock in the cave ceiling, he heard another roar coming from deeper inside the cave. Why was he making so much noise? Could it be that Krolion was still in pain after Jess hit him with the special trident? If he was still in pain, this meant that it would be easier to kill him.

They went further into the cave and found a massive cavern the size of the castle of Railux. There were so many rocks that came in all shapes and sizes. There was a particularly massive hump in the ground that didn't seem to belong there because of the unusual cracks in the ground. Catastrophe knew this trick- camouflaging with your surroundings. He told the Aquarions to surround the hump and get ready to throw at his command.

"Throw!" shouted Catastrophe. The Aquarions threw their spears at the hump and soon it was covered in hundreds of tridents. Krolion was bound to be dead. Suddenly, A deep ominous voice came from the cavern ceiling.

"Did you bring any spares?" Said the voice. It was Krolion. He was watching the Aquarion army all this time while they stupidly threw their tridents on some mound of rock. Catastrophe also knew this trick- making your opponents use up all of their equipment on a fake camouflaged version of you and then attacking them with the element of surprise while the opponents were left defenceless. But where was the element of surprise? Krolion gave away his location willingly. Krolion then snapped his fingers and this time, it wasn't the octosharks but these invisible mimic octopuses who could use their retro reflective pigments in their skin to camouflage extremely well with their surroundings and they could shape-shift as well so they could look like any animal. They grabbed many Aquarions and held them back from using their weapons. Jess tried to pull one off Captain Catastrophe and the octopus left immediately. It was the

Fire Stone! It heated the octopus' arm so much that it let go. Jess went and helped get the octopi arms off the Aquarion soldiers.

Catastrophe could add another trick to his book of tricks now- when a giant octopus dragon monster sends their camouflaging octopuses after your army, make sure you have a girl next to you who can remove the tentacles of those octopuses and save your army.

Catastrophe didn't throw his trident at the rock but held onto it. He looked at Krolion straight into his glowing red eyes and threw the trident. It flew into Krolion's massive hand but he caught it and tried to snap it in two but couldn't as the trident was extremely strong. Krolion jumped down from the cave ceiling and created a small shockwave that pushed everyone away from Krolion. Jess advanced towards Krolion holding the fire crystal. She then gave her punch all she had as she punched Krolion so hard he fell over. That fire crystal was really powerful. Jess was literally boiling in the water!

"I was going easy on you, now the real fight begins!" Krolion sent thousands of octosharks and Catastrophe presumed that they were only a distraction as they were fighting the Aquarions but the real target was Krolion. Catastrophe was defenceless without a weapon. This was really Jess's fight.

Jess had a forcefield of bubbles around her, maybe because the fire crystal was powered by Jess's anger was why it turned on. Krolion grabbed Jess with his extending tentacles and tossed her against the wall, leaving a crater behind. Jess lifted up a massive rock and threw it at Krolion. The rock exploded upon impact and stunned Krolion.

"ARGHH" shouted Krolion. He swam towards Jess and grabbed her with his massive hand and swam out of the cave with immense speed, past the soldiers who were outside the cave and launched out of the water into the outside town of Aquarion. Most citizens have never seen Krolion in the flesh and he was much bigger than they expected.

Krolion held Jess up to his face and said, "You are going to be sorry that Neptune sent you and your puny army to fight me." Krolion leaned back and threw Jess into a nearby house, leaving a gaping hole inside it. Krolion then crushed houses with his feet and killed people with his tentacles. The overground soldiers shot multiple arrows from their ballistas which impaled Krolion's back and he roared in pain. His wings opened up and flapped madly to create an artificial hurricane which pushed the soldiers and their ballistas back. Krolion advanced out of Aquarion and attempted to take out the defences at the front of the kingdom where they posed the strongest threat to him.

Suddenly there was a blindingly bright light that shone from the ground, but Krolion ignored it as he thought it was a reflection from the sun. But then he noticed cracks in the ground widening and then he felt the ground getting hotter and hotter.

Krolion squinted and looked carefully at the cracks in the ground- there was a person in there! "NO! IT CAN'T BE!" exclaimed Krolion. It was Jess! She was still alive and she was flaming with anger-quite literally as well. Flames erupted from the cracks, burning Krolion's wings. He roared in pain and then the ground was breaking into pieces. The people of Aquarion were already moving further in towards the kingdom so they were safe, but the explosions and roars didn't comfort them at all.

Krolion lost his balance as the cracks widened even further, revealing a lake of hot rocks and lava below. Krolion couldn't fly, this was the end for him. Krolion fell halfway into the holes below but he still was grabbing on. At last, the pressure from the magma below was released as a huge eruption, vaporising Krolion almost instantly. A great sound was heard from the depths of the castle:

BOOOOOMM!

CHAPTER 10

THE CRYSTAL OF WATER

"What was that?" Said Catastrophe, who was inside the cave with the Aquarions fighting the army of octosharks. Jess was taken outside the cave by Krolion but the soldiers could have stopped Krolion. But what could create the explosion? The self destruct button? No. Catastrophe still had it and if it was activated everyone would die. Catastrophe took one of the tridents left in the water and wrangled an octoshark so he could get out of the cave quickly.

The soldiers who were meant to be outside the cave weren't there anymore. What happened to them? Suddenly the octoshark sped up and up and soon enough, it threw him of its back and Catastrophe was caught in a current that led him back to over-ground Aquarion. He then flew out of the hole and face planted the muddy floor. Everyone was cheering for some reason. Were they laughing at him?

If they were, then they were facing the wrong way.

Catastrophe got up and wiped the mud off his face. He could see something heading towards him, it was a pair of legs but it looked like they were on fire. They suddenly turned into normal human legs. He looked up and saw a woman, who held out her hand and pulled Catastrophe to his feet.

"Jess?" said Catastrophe, "What just happened? Is Krolion dead?"

"Yes I'm alright, thanks for asking" Jess responded sarcastically.

"Sorry, I'm just so confused about what happened, did we get the water crystal?"

"Oh no! I forgot!" cried Jess. "Let's go and check the area, the crystal of water is light blue and glows like an aurora. If it's near water it is said that it will make strange shapes and patterns in the water such as whirlpools."

They searched high and low for the crystal. Catastrophe saw a strange pattern in the water that he thought was probably sticks arranged in such a way that it looked like a group of strange shapes.

"Jess I think I found it!" said Catastrophe as he moved towards the water. There was something floating in the water! It was the crystal of water, and Catastrophe reached out for it as it was on the edge of the lake. The crystal was glowing like an aurora, like King Neptune's lost son. Then it clicked: was Neptune's son the water crystal? Could something have gone wrong with Krolion extracting the water crystal energy from Neptune's son?

Jess arrived, and said, "It makes sense! Neptune's son was never seen. Do you think we can reverse the transformation?"

"I doubt it, Krolion is dead."

"Yeah, you're right." Captain Catastrophe reluctantly answered. How were they supposed to break the heartbreaking news to King Neptune? They just had to deliver it.

"Wait a second, do you know where King Neptune was taken? Remember, he was injured in that attack from Krolion" said Jess.

"You're right, we don't know where he is but we could ask some people where the treatment centre is. They should know." Captain Catastrophe and Jess walked back through the waterfall of Aquarion and it looked nothing like it did before; smashed houses, burning bits of rubble and wood, bodies splayed out on the muddy floor. Even though this was the decoy city, lots of damage had been done to the actual castle of Aquarion. It was over. Krolion may have lost, but in the eyes of the people, he won.

They soon found the treatment centre by following the few remaining soldiers carrying their dead comrades on nets. It was horrible in there, people were screaming, shouting and pleading the healers to end their lives. They found the king, who looked even worse than he did when he got hit with the massive pile of rubble. How were they going to tell him?

"Catastrophe?, Jess?, is that you?" Said the king, weakly, lying down on the bed.

" Your Majesty, we did it, we killed Krolion." Said Catastrophe.

"I knew you could do it, ever since I met you, I knew you could take him on. Jess, you fought extremely well and without you, Krolion would have killed us all. I know you didn't find my son. But how can I repay you for trying to find him? I have tried to get into Krolion's lair hundreds of times but I still failed, yet you have tried once and got in. I don't want to live anymore without my son or my wife. It's time I meet them. Before I... go...," King Neptune gestured towards Catastrophe, asking him to come further.

"My final wish and order of King Neptune I of Aquarion is... that... you... will be... the next...king... of A.q..uarion..." He closed his eyes and whispered, " Hail Aquarion" and fell silent.

Catastrophe and Jess walked out, in silence.

CHAPTER 11

THE JOURNEY CONTINUES

Catastrophe took the water crystal with him. He couldn't speak to Jess, let alone face her. From the corner of his eye, could have sworn he saw a tear on Jess's cheek.

Catastrophe and Jess walked out of the hospital and as they opened the grand doors into the open, they saw every single citizen standing outside waiting for news of the king.

Catastrophe took his hat off, and slowly announced, "The king.... Is dead." Gasps and screams were heard amongst the crowd. Soldiers knelt in honour of the king. "The king was extremely unwell after that ambush by Kroli- The monster. For your knowledge, the monster is dead. The king wanted you to know that your new king is... me. I know many of you may have doubts about me, but there is a kingdom called Railux. There are many opportunities for you there and my friend, Jess is the princess of Railux. A crow has been sent to Railux regarding the situation and I'm sure the King will welcome you kindly. Take the horses in your stables and ride to Railux as soon as you have collected every necessity from your houses. Good luck." The crowd then dispersed into what was left of their houses and the whole town.

Catastrophe could see something in the distance; it was a crow painted red and white. It was painted red and white because that's Railux's colours and many other kingdoms would do the same to prevent confusion between whose crow was whose. It slowed down and landed on Catastrophe's arm with a small piece of rolled up parchment attached to its leg. Catastrophe took the parchment and rolled it out flat. The message said, 'Captain, that is fine, they will have enough places to live and we have started building a new village. I'm assuming you have at least two crystals? Write back to me and send the message on the same crow. Regards, King Tyger'.

Catastrophe wrote back, 'Your Majesty, I have arranged for the citizens to collect their belongings and make their way on their horses to Railux. And yes, we have the fire and water crystals. We are aiming to get the crystal of Earth now. Good luck.' Catastrophe tied the parchment to the crow's leg and then the crow flew back in the direction it came from.

Catastrophe then held the Water crystal up to his face. It looked very similar to the fire crystal, in terms of the structure. But the Fire crystal was more sharp edged. The water crystal had round edges and felt quite cold. Inside the crystal, there was a slow, reanimated, aurora-like pattern. It was very mesmerising to look at.

He then felt a tap on his back, he turned around expecting to see Jess, but instead saw a small child. The child said, "Please can you help me find my mother?, We got separated in the crowd."

"Sure kid," said Catastrophe, "before we look for your mother, you look really exhausted! Let's have a drink and freshen up by the river."

Catastrophe and the child walked to the river, which was only about 30 feet away from them. Catastrophe put the water crystal in his pocket and then scooped up some water. He splashed it on the child"s face to clean it. "Does that feel better?" inquired Catastrophe.

"Yeah!" The child tried to scoop up some water with his small hands but couldn't get a good hold of the water. Catastrophe then felt a sudden shock of cold in his pocket. The water crystal! He took it out and this time it was glowing much faster than it did before. Then, out of the river, a small fountain of water shot up. The child put his mouth under it and drank the water, relinquishing his thirst.

"Woah" muttered Catastrophe. The water crystal was just as powerful as the fire crystal. The crystal seemed to have bonded with Catastrophe, because the crystal knew that Catastrophe needed a way to give the boy some water!

Catastrophe took the boy back to his mother who was in one of the few houses that were still standing. He then rolled out his map and crossed out the water crystal, which was dotted on the map. He and Jess only knew where 4 crystals were, but there were 5. As Jeffrey(the poor traveller who gave the information about the crystals to Catastrophe and Jess but died shortly after) said that no one knows where the 5th crystal was.

"Looks like we're heading for Nazura, the land where nature is in charge."

"Jess! We're going to Nazura!" Shouted Catastrophe. With the water and fire crystal, they should have a decent chance against the infamous monster; Grokan. Grokan was the only reason no person left Nazura alive. He could control nature and no one knows what he looked like, how big he was or how powerful he was because as no one left Nazura alive, so they couldn't tell anyone.

As Jess went back to get Catastrophe's and her horses, Catastrophe thought about the next battle. With no army, and barely any information about Nazura, he and Jess were going to have to learn how to harness the full power of their crystals. Jess was more used to her crystal as she had more experience with the Fire crystal. It was obviously going to take a long time for Captain Catastrophe to bond with the water crystal even more.

Jess returned with the horses. Catastrophe had one last look at Aquarion while the remaining citizens were thanking them for their help. Luckily, Railux had enough accommodation for Aquarion's citizens. Catastrophe announced, "We shall leave now, it's been a pleasure to defend your kingdom against the monster. Here's the map to Railux. I wish you a safe journey!"

CHAPTER 12

NAZURA

Catastrophe and Jess rode off to Nazura. On the way, a conversation started.

"What can the water crystal do?" inquired Jess.

"Nothing much, so far I have learned to make a fountain appear out of nowhere."

"I also haven't learned much."

"Are you kidding me? You could break the ground, barely feel any pain and walk away untouched!"

"Okay, Okay! When I did do that, I don't know what triggered it. It could have been my anger that powered the crystal."

Something sparked in Catastrophe's head. "That's it! It's our bonds with the crystals that strengthen our powers! I only just bonded with my crystal so the power was quite weak, and that's why I was only able to make a small fountain. You however, had the crystal for much longer and that's why you were a lot stronger than me. I think we are worthy of our crystals!"

"How long did it take you to work that out?"

"I guessed. It's a common thing now- I do something or say something really great and it turns out it was accidentally said."

Jess laughed out loud. She then said, "That wasn't an accident."

Catastrophe was silent after that.

After that conversation, they stopped at one of the markets that were on the path to Nazura and resupplied. They used up nearly all their supplies at Aquarion. One of the people who worked at the markets recognised Catastrophe. When Catastrophe was buying some water from him, the person said, "Hey, aren't you that guy who killed that monster in Chailium?"

"How do you know that?" responded Catastrophe, with a confused face.

"Because everyone knows about you! You two killed Morphon, the special monster that lived in the castle of Chailium! When you broke out, the king sent many soldiers after you but you left on your horses so quickly that the soldiers didn't know where you went! The king even placed a bounty on you worth 1,000 gold coins!" Catastrophe started backing away, afraid that the man would try and catch him and Jess.

"No no no, I'm not going to take you to the king, I know what he does is cruel so I'll let you go! Plus if you guys could take down a monster, then it would cost you no trouble to deal with me!" he laughed.

"Thank you," Said Jess. If the man did decide to take them to the king of Chailium, Jess had other plans for the man.

They left the markets and the sun was setting in front of them. They observed the sunset at the horizon, spreading its sunlight into the sky. Rich streaks of red blended with oranges and purples. The sun cast its golden rays down upon the clouds, turning them bright red.

"Beautiful, isn't it?" sighed Jess, who was quite tired after their adventurous day. She laid down on the back of her horse, and stretched her arms. Catastrophe was still dwelling on the fact that there was a bounty on their heads, but how could he bring it up now, especially in this amazing moment?

They had to get the tents up as the sky was getting darker. After Catastrophe and Jess got the tents and campfire up, it was night. The last moments of the setting sun disappeared over the horizon, the hues giving way to a dusty purple scattered with the glitter of a faraway star. The distant skyline stood silhouetted against a velvety sky and the relatively bright dusk was enveloped by the twilight sky.

The fire crackled in the middle of the campsite, projecting long shadows in the surrounding area. The light cast by the flames curled in strange shapes and were providing a small radius of light. The fire was pulsing, the glowing embers seemed to move in a pattern with the flames. It was mesmerising to watch. It stood out like a sore thumb in the night. It was as comforting as it was warm.

Catastrophe then closed his eyes and fell asleep.

The next day, Captain Catastrophe woke up and it was raining.

"Ugh" groaned Catastrophe, who was soaking. Jess didn't need to be woken up because she also woke up in the same state as Catastrophe.

We're literally in the open fields here!, how are we supposed to find shelter?!" Shouted Catastrophe. The distant trees were writhing and flailing, Rain hammered the ground, like bullets. Coal black clouds readied up like a cobra readying itself for an attack. They sprayed lightning mercilessly onto the pitiful scene below, which slashed through the sky.

Jess shouted back, " Hang on, I think I got something!" She took out her fire crystal and chanted, "Fire shield!" A ball of fire appeared around them, protecting them from the constant rain shower. Catastrophe sighed, "Phew, it's so warm in here." And then the rain started to break the shield, as you know; water puts out fire. What were they supposed to do now?

Catastrophe had a brilliant idea. He got the water crystal out and chanted the same thing as Jess, but instead said, "Water Shield!" This time they couldn't see anything, but they could feel no rain! The water shield stopped the rain from reaching them! Jess started a small campfire within the shield by simply pointing at the few bundle of sticks.

"Wow!" Exclaimed Jess, "I think you have begun to bond with your crystal!"

"We should probably wait the rain out. I don't think the shield moves in sync with us, that will take a lot more time and concentration to achieve that."

"Yeah, it will. But you'll do it." Said Jess.

Abruptly, they could hear something out of sync with the rain, it sounded like galloping. There were 5 horses with riders. One in the front, three in the middle and one in the back. The one at the back was carrying a flag. Jess couldn't make out the flag that well, but it alarmingly looked like the flag of Chailium! The king of Chailium had sent soldiers to every main kingdom to search for them!

"There's no cover here! When they see the tents they're going to come over here!" Whispered Jess. They waited for the soldiers, wondering if they would notice the tents in this kind of weather. It was really hard to see through the rain but they would easily notice two brightly coloured tents and the campfire.

They waited, and waited. The soldiers got closer and closer. Catastrophe drew out his golden pistol and loaded it. Jess got her sword out. Things were about to get hairy. The soldiers still hadn't seen them but one of them finally shouted, "Look ere. Looks like someone set up some tents and camped here. Let's see if anyone's still there." The soldiers got down from their horses and walked towards the tents.

Catastrophe was about to get up until Jess pulled on his arm.

"Jess, what are you doing?" whispered Catastrophe, clearly confused and annoyed.

"Didn't you notice, they would have spotted us by now because your legs are clearly not behind the tent." And Jess was right. Catastrophe's legs were not hidden, so why couldn't the soldiers see them?

"Are we somehow invisible? The water could be refracting the light so the soldiers can't see my legs in clarity!"

"You know, that could actually be happening!" said Jess. The soldier then turned towards the tent and shouted, "They're over ere'!"

"Uh… do we run or attack? The fire crystal doesn't work at its best in water and I just ran out of my water powers. My gun is probably jammed from the amount of water that's in it." Asked Catastrophe, who was quite timid.

"Do you have a sword?" Asked Jess. The soldiers were advancing.

"Yeah" responded Catastrophe, who was getting ready for a fight.

"Attack."

They rolled out and in synchronization, plunged their swords into the first man. Blood gushed out, turning the black, mushy mud below into a horrid, devilish-red-like mud. The man fell to his knees and then fell into the red mud, face first. Catastrophe flailed about for the man's rifle while Jess advanced towards the other men.

Jess noticed the two men in front of her were waiting for her to make the first move. Jess waited, and then a strike of lightning flashed before the soldiers eyes. Jess used the lightning as a distraction and rolled forward, slashed the first man and then the second fell soon after. There were two men left. One had a pistol and shot. The bullet travelled towards Jess and while Jess dodged that one, the other man shot his pistol and the bullet was lodged in her leg. She wailed for a moment and then kept quiet. She clearly didn't want to be assumed that she was weak.

The man walked towards Jess, ready to take his shot. Then, out of the blue, Catastrophe arrived and shot both men with the shotgun he spent about 5 minutes loading. Jess smiled and lied down.

"Water shield!" The same shield generated around them and Catastrophe lifted Jess up and carried her over to the tents where he washed the wound and patched it up. Jess was quite lucky as the bullet grazed her leg. She could walk just fine but she rode on the horse to make sure no further damage was done to the wound.

They carried on to Nazura and the rain had stopped now. They started to notice the path on which they rode on was starting to look more natural and many flowers started to bloom as they rode past them. They were on the official path of Nazura. The trees formed a tunnel with their overhanging branches interlocking with each other. This meant that Nazura was close, really close.

"Jess, how's your leg holding up?"

"It's fine, I'm pretty sure I can walk now." They were so close to Nazura that they wouldn't be surprised if they were there already. Suddenly, a roar was emitted from the end of the 'tunnel'.

"That doesn't sound good." said Jess. That roar could have been from Grokan. This time, fighting Grokan with the crystals would finish him off quicker but no one knew of Grokan's powers, which could lead to serious danger if they underestimated him.

Catastrophe's horse and Jess's horse came to a sudden halt. Why did they stop? Were they scared?

"Jess, I think we're here." The horses were obviously scared of something up ahead. They then heard some strange humming from the same area where they heard the roaring from. Their horses then slowly turned their heads towards Catastrophe and Jess. For some reason, they had a slight menacing look about them.

"Jess? Something doesn't seem right."

The humming at the end of the tunnel changed tone and then the horses' heads were shaking uncontrollably.

"Run!" Shouted Jess. The horses were chasing them! Their weapons were on the horses saddlebags.

"Catastrophe! Don't you have that shotgun you stole from that soldier?"

"I can't Jess, they're not doing this on purpose."

"We don't have a choice! Do it!" shouted Jess.

Catastrophe whispered "I'm sorry" and was about to aim his shotgun at the horses until they stopped dead and dropped to the floor. There was no blood. Something powerful had possessed them and killed them using only its mental powers. Jess was frozen in shock and bewilderment out of what she had witnessed.

“I didn’t know Grokan was capable of that!” exclaimed Jess, who was still shocked.

“There’s probably more on the way” said Catastrophe. Were the power of the crystals going to be enough? They’ll have to see.

As the pair got closer to the tunnel, more strange noises could be heard. They were like human screams but somehow sounded ten times more terrifying than it should sound. “Those aren’t reassuring sounds.” quietly said Jess. Catastrophe, who was silent, wanted to get away from this place.

Suddenly, an extremely slender green hand stretched out of the tunnel and tried to grab Catastrophe and Jess.

“Jess, RUN!” shouted Catastrophe, who was also running extremely fast. However the hand was moving at an inexplicable speed and lunged for Catastrophe’s cape. It grabbed it and pulled on it, causing Catastrophe to fall face first on to the ground.

“OWWWWW!!!!!!” Exclaimed Catastrophe, who reckoned he had a broken nose. “Go Jess!, Don’t look back!” as Catastrophe was dragged further into the tunnel.

CHAPTER 13

THE LAIR OF GROKAN

Catastrophe was still being dragged into the tunnel, unaware about how long he was being dragged for. When he came to a sudden halt, he felt very weak and could not get up. There was no more light in the tunnel of trees, just darkness. Catastrophe was crawling away from wherever he was but then, a ring of fire appeared around the area he was in. It turned out Catastrophe was in a cavern, infested with every type of tree and plant. Waterfalls were at every corner of the cavern. Catastrophe then tried to get up but tripped himself up and fell again. He took his water crystal out and whispered, "water shield." The shield formed around Catastrophe and he thought that wherever he was, there was no easy way of getting out. There was a large rock formation on the top, it was very large and didn't seem like it should've been there. Catastrophe then squinted and realised that the rock formation on the top of the cavern was much bigger than he first thought it was. The rock formation looked like it was breathing, because it was slowly rising up and then fell slowly as well.

Catastrophe then gained enough strength to get up and then walked towards the middle of the cavern he was in. Suddenly, the rock started juddering and created vibrations that shook the whole cavern. Was the water shield still on? Catastrophe checked and it wasn't on. The rock formation then fell off the cavern ceiling and Catastrophe had to get out of the way. Dodging the other pieces of debris falling in front of Catastrophe, he ran and hid behind a boulder that was fixed in the ground.

The rock formation plummeted towards the ground and shook the cavern. It then, shockingly started rolling on its own. It then adjusted its posture and now it was shaking again, this time it looked like it was shaving off excess rocks and moss that had grown on it. Even though Catastrophe didn't want to assume it looked like an animal now, it very much looked like one. Catastrophe reassured himself that a rock clearly couldn't hurt him. It was at that specific moment where large pieces of rock started folding out, revealing a 200ft, four legged, stone armoured creature.

"Are you Grokan?!" Shouted Catastrophe, wanting to peacefully approach the monster. Suddenly, the monster brought down his fist causing a shockwave that lifted Catastrophe off his feet and flung him across half the cavern floor. Catastrophe screamed in pain.The monster then opened its mouth to roar but no sound came out. It seemed like the monster noticed something from the mouth of the cave in which Catastrophe was brought in.

A ball of fire shot out of the cave, curling its way towards the monster and hit it on the side of its belly, causing it to fall down. Jess was here! He had to get to her, for his safety. Catastrophe made his way towards the cave but it was quite a long distance away because he was on the other side of the cavern. As he was running, he thought that this monster was Grokan and probably ouldn't speak English unsurprisingly because it didn't answer when Catastrophe asked him if he was Grokan. Nonetheless, if Catastrophe didn't do anything, he would be dead. Jess was getting closer because the light from the tunnel was getting brighter.

More balls of fire shot out of the tunnel like a cannonball, impaling Grokan as some rocks chipped off and fell on the floor. The floor was literally littered with coals. Grokan then ripped the rocks of his face revealing his eyes and mouth. His eyes were made of fire and they were two diagonal lines that intersected each other in the middle of his face. His jaw was coloured in some sort of lava-red residue.

Catastrophe was nearly at the tunnel until he saw Grokan chasing him! Grokan let out a deafening roar and then started speeding up. Catastrophe could hear Grokan's footsteps getting louder and louder. Grokan was going to catch up with him soon. What was he going to do? Catastrophe got the water crystal out and without knowing what to do, braced himself and whispered to the crystal, "Please protect me." Grokan slammed his large, rocky fist on Catastrophe.

When Grokan lifted his fist off the ground he expected to see bloody remains of Catastrophe but there was nothing there apart from a puddle. The puddle risen up and formed itself into a human shape; Catastrophe survived! The water crystal had listened to him and turned him into water so that he was technically invincible to physical attacks. Grokan's shoulders started rumbling and two black spikes came out of his back.They fired at Catastrophe. The first one went straight through his head but because he was made of water, the spike just impaled the ground behind him.

The second spike impaled the ground below Catastrophe, hoping to make him fall into the emptiness below as the ground opened up. The Water crystal had a few more tricks up its vertex though. When the ground opened up, Catastrophe disappeared. But he didn't go down, in fact he was floating in the air but not visible to the naked eye as he had just turned himself into water vapour. Catastrophe was technically flying! "Woah!' Was all he could say, but he had to get to Jess.

Catastrophe headed towards the cave in which Jess was in. He could see the cave but he was also finding out ways they could defeat Grokan. Grokan was extremely powerful and if he had a target, he would definitely not hesitate to destroy it. Catastrophe and Jess would have to use 'the element of surprise' to attack him. Grokan was massive; about 200ft in height and about 100ft long. This meant he couldn't have much manoeuvrability. Catastrophe and Jess were small and had the elements of Fire and Water on their side. They could move much quicker and would be more agile than Grokan.

Catastrophe arrived at the cave entrance and saw Jess throwing hundreds of fireballs as she was advancing towards the entrance of Nazura. Catastrophe was still water vapour so Jess couldn't see him. Catastrophe then tried to say, "Jess!" without scaring her but when he did, Jess was startled so much she fired a massive fire ball behind her back to make sure no one was there. Catastrophe then calmed her down by saying, "Jess, it's me! Catastrophe! I'm invisible because the water crystal has turned me into water vapour! Hang on, let me turn myself back to normal..."

This time, Catastrophe didn't have to tell the crystal anything, he somehow thought about what he wanted to do and the Water crystal did it! Their bond was definitely getting stronger. Catastrophe had returned to his normal self and he checked his body to see if he was missing any parts. Nope, all parts were there!

Surprisingly, Jess hugged Catastrophe tightly and said, "Are you okay?"

"Yep, I'm fine! A few bruises here and there but all good."

"So, how are we going to take down Grokan? He seems to be very persistent." said Jess, who looked exhausted. Grokan wasn't going to give up easily. Catastrophe suggested making the ground below Grokan weak so Grokan would hopefully fall into a hole. Jess agreed with this plan. She clenched her fists and prepared a huge, elephant-sized fireball and blasted it out of the cave.

Jess aimed the fireball at Grokan's underbelly; the least protected part of his body. However, Grokan opened his mouth and created a tornado that was pulling Jess's fireball's into his mouth. Soon, Grokan was pulling Jess in! She tried to fight it, but Grokan's power was too much. Jess was about to get sucked in!

Suddenly, one of the waterfalls in the corner started acting strange. It wasn't falling but heading in Grokan's direction, hitting him in the back. This caused Grokan to look away for a few seconds, granting Jess a chance to strike. When she clenched her fist though, nothing happened. It's like she lost her powers! Jess then felt herself falling, and she was falling faster and faster until she fell on something cushioning and comfortable-water. Catastrophe's water crystal had summoned a water cushion so Jess would be okay.

Catastrophe was at the end of the tunnel, controlling the waterfalls and trying to keep Grokan off Jess. Catastrophe used the water to bring Jess towards him.

"Jess! Are you okay?"

"Yeah I'm fine, however I can't use my powers; it seems Grokan has taken them from me and if you look at the Fire crystal, it's not as red or bright as it used to be." She held her hand out and she was right, the fire crystal was a dark maroon colour. And when Jess tried to activate the Fire crystal, nothing happened.

"Okay, because you clearly aren't in a state to fight Grokan, I'll take care of him."

Catastrophe would have to take care of this battle now. He felt a different sort of energy surging through him; he felt himself getting taller as he saw the ground becoming smaller and smaller until he came to a stop; he was enormous! Thanks to the water crystal, he became a giant made out of water! This battle going to be interesting

Grokan got up, but this time he was acting different; spikes started to grow out of his body, making his back impenetrable. He then stomped towards the colossal water giant; Catastrophe. Catastrophe took a chunk of a cliff he was next to, held it for a few seconds and turned it into eroded rock using hydraulic action from his hand made of water. He then released the dust at Grokan, who was heading for Catastrophe. The dust blinded Grokan, but he was still heading towards Catastrophe. Catastrophe got out of the way causing Grokan to crash into the cliff side. This would have made him extremely dizzy. Catastrophe aimed a punch at Grokan's head and when his 50 tonne force of water hit Grokan's paper jaw, Grokan fell once again with such force that the whole cavern shook.

Because of the amount of bangs and crashes in the cavern, the cavern was becoming unstable and Jess started noticing this. She couldn't alert Catastrophe because she couldn't fly nor could Catastrophe hear her from this distance. She tried to find a route to get near Catastrophe. She could see a few ledges that she could climb pretty easily. She started climbing the cliff, hoping she would get to Catastrophe in time.

Catastrophe lunged forward to grab Grokan by the back. Grokan's back, which was covered in spikes shot outwards, penetrating Catastrophe's body but going straight through as his body was made of water. One of the spikes which flew past Catastrophe's ear was caught by him. He threw it back at Grokan's naked back. Catastrophe expected the fight to end here but the spike exploded upon impact. Grokan was unharmed. Catastrophe was very confused, why did Grokan not die?

Ah, his stone plated armour! Catastrophe had to break it. Using water at different temperatures would break the stone. Catastrophe tried to send a telepathic message to the Water crystal saying, I need hot water," and surprisingly it worked as Catastrophe could see his own hand steaming. Grokan advanced towards Catastrophe, even angrier than before and when Grokan lashed his tail at Catastrophe, he jumped over the tail and when he landed on the unstable cavern floor, he smashed his boiling fist into Grokan's stone armoured back. Grokan roared in pain, but his stone armour was still intact. Catastrophe then got his left hand out, which was made of cold water, clenched it and smashed it into Grokan's back. Grokan was in even more pain, but the stone armour was still intact!

Catastrophe picked up one of the spikes that came from Grokan's back, which was lying on the floor. He then tightened his grip in the spike, aiming it at Grokan's back and threw it. The spike arced in the air, and then striking down into Grokan's stone armoured back. The spike exploded into bits and so did Grokan's armour. They fell on the ground, causing even more instability in the cavern. Jess was climbing the cliffside and this shaking wasn't doing any good for her as the ledges were vibrating with such force her feet fell many times but somehow she still held on with her rough hands.

Catastrophe shouted, "Have you had enough?! We can talk this out!" But Grokan didn't have enough. Even though it looked like he was battered and nearly finished, he charged towards Catastrophe. He had enough of this battle. It was time to end this.

As Grokan was charging head-first, when he got close to Catastrophe, Catastrophe grasped Grokan's head and was drowning him with his giant water hands. Grokan tried to resist but he was too weak. Suddenly a bright green flash of light exploded from within Grokan. Catastrophe stumbled backwards and fell on the cracked, damaged cavern floor. Catastrophe could feel himself getting closer to the cavern floor; he assumed he was falling but he was just shrinking back to normal size.

The green light was flashing so bright, it knocked Jess off the ledge and she fell from a height about 25ft. She expected to break her spine when she hit the ground but Catastrophe caught her with his last ounces of power. She was brought to Catastrophe and they both marvelled at the flash of light from Grokan. Soon, Grokan's body decomposed like Morphon's body revealing just a bright green light.

As they squinted, they realised that the thing inside that was flashing was the Earth crystal.

CHAPTER 14

THE CRYSTAL OF EARTH

Catastrophe wasn't sure how long the crystal of Earth was going to be floating in the air, but they needed to get under it so they could catch it. The cavern was going to collapse any minute so this was their only chance. Catastrophe and Jess ran towards the crystal, dodging falling debris from the ceiling. The light from the crystal was fading away, which could mean that the crystal of Earth was about to fall. They picked up their pace and noticed that the cavern floor was breaking apart like tectonic plates. Vast, empty, jet black holes started popping up every few seconds.

The crystal stopped flashing now and it was visible from where Catastrophe and Jess were. They realised that the crystal was about to fall now so Catastrophe boosted Jess by giving her a jump lift. This way, she jumped over some large rocks that were in her way and got to the crystal faster. However, when she landed on the fragile floor, she caused a crack to seep its way towards her and open up, nearly swallowing her. She was directly under the crystal now and was ready to catch it.

Catastrophe also got there but when he landed on the ground he caused the ground to open up, causing Jess to fall into the gap but Catastrophe held on to her. The crystal then fell; Catastrophe tried to catch it but if he let go of the edge he was holding on he would fall along with Jess into the empty darkness. However, when the crystal fell, Catastrophe swung Jess towards the crystal so she could catch it.

The crystal fell into Jess's palm and put it in her pocket. So, they got the crystal, but how were they supposed to get out? Catastrophe asked Jess to give her other hand and she was on the cavern floor again. Jess handed over the crystal to Catastrophe saying, "You earned it." Catastrophe would spend some time looking at the crystal but their lives were in danger as the cavern was collapsing.

Catastrophe then felt a small tingle in his pocket; The Earth crystal? He took it out, clenched it and started pulsating green. Catastrophe looked up as the cavern ceiling and noticed a vine dropped from the ceiling. He grabbed it and so did Jess. The vine then pulled them up, dodging the falling rocks and dirt that kept on coming until they blasted out the ceiling. It was the end of Nazura as it was falling apart. It was time to leave.

CHAPTER 15

A CHANGE IN PLAN

The strange vine seemed to have taken them to an open field that was unusually far away from where Grokan's lair was. Catastrophe took out the Earth crystal and looked at it very closely; he could notice that inside there was something inside it. As he squinted, he noticed that there was a setting inside and it looked like Nazura before it was destroyed. Catastrophe gave the crystal to Jess and she looked through it as well.

"Wow! This crystal was the centrepiece of Nazura, I think the crystal was the reason Nazura was around for so long."

"Not a bad theory, what do you think the crystal can do?"

"Well," Jess have the crystal back to Catastrophe, "before we look into that, we need some form of transport, and since we're in an empty field with no animals in sight, we need to get looking."

"You could use your fire crystal though right?"

"For what? We'll need to find some signs of a market nearby. We'll need to split up and search!"

Catastrophe sighed, "Well, we need horses and there are none in plain sight; and we are in an empty field so how could we possibly find some?"

"Shut up and just keep looking!" Shouted Jess, who was irritated. As she was walking along the small slopes of luscious green grass, she started growing feelings for Catastrophe. He was very kind to Jess, and never got angry with her. Sure he was a bit clumsy, but that's his character. She felt quite sorry for shouting on Catastrophe. Even though Jess was extremely brave, she couldn't bring herself to talk to Catastrophe about her feelings as she believed Catastrophe wouldn't understand. Regardless, she carried on.

Catastrophe, while looking for a horse, was also fixing his eyes on the Earth crystal, looking around in mini Nazura. Suddenly, the crystal flashed green and blinded Catastrophe. He fell back, still holding the crystal and hit the wet grass, but it felt as hard as rock as Catastrophe fell on his head. He then blacked out.

He then felt some kind of wet material on his face, he woke up and saw a horse, staring at him from upside down. He forced the horse's head off him and stood up, amazed to find a horse when a minute ago, there were no animals at all. However, that wasn't the thing that intrigued Catastrophe. The fact that the horse had somehow found Catastrophe without any help was quite strange. What was also strange was that the horse was extremely friendly as when it woke Catastrophe up it was licking him like a good dog would.

Catastrophe knew all sorts of crystals such as the fire or water crystal had powers that would make phenomenons happen so was this a sign of what the Earth crystal could do? Anyways, having put that thought aside for now, he called over Jess.

"Hey Jess! I found a horse... well it actually found me!"

"What!?" Questioned Jess, who didn't understand what Catastrophe was saying.

"Just come up here and I'll explain it to you!" After Catastrophe explained the short story to Jess she was as confused as Catastrophe was.

"It's probably the first sign of bonding with the Earth crystal?" Suggested Jess.

"Hmm... You could be right, however I was expecting the crystal to make a plant grow out of the grass or something... Hang on a second!" As soon Catastrophe said this, a small plant pushed through the small blades of the grass, rising higher and higher until it reached the height of his knee. Catastrophe knelt down to observe the plant and he noticed it was a flower as it was blooming. Jess also knelt down to look at the plant and could see purple petals folding out gracefully. The golden pollen was dotted on three small strings that nearly dropped over the flower itself.

Catastrophe and Jess were very close together. In fact, they were so close together, Jess could notice the small stitches on Catastrophe's brown, dirty clothes. Jess thought about telling Catastrophe about how she felt about him but as she finally picked up the courage to tell him, Catastrophe stood up and walked over to the friendly horse, unaware that he ruined Jess's opportunity.

"Another time, Jess," she said to herself.

"Okay, what's the next crystal?" Asked Catastrophe.

"Well, there are five crystals; Fire, Water, Earth, Air and the unknown fifth one. We know nothing about the fifth crystal, but the map my father gave me has a pattern on it."

"What kind of pattern?"

"If you look carefully, the kingdom of Railux is in the middle of the map, and the four crystals that are pointed on the map are an equal distance apart from each other. The crystals are also the same distance from Railux castle so if you draw a line from the crystals connecting to Railux castle they form the four points of a star."

"Aha! So the last crystal should be in this lower portion of the map as that's where the fifth point of the star should be!"

"Exactly. Now the only decision we have to make here is; which crystal are we going to get? We know where the Air crystal is, so it's wiser to get the air crystal before getting the last crystal we know nothing about."

Catastrophe agreed and Jess gave the map back to Catastrophe. As Catastrophe looked at the map one more time he wiped off some of the dust and grime that was on there and realised that the crystal of air was actually on an island and the dust was covering the expanse of ocean between the mainland and the island.

"Uhhh… Jess?"

"Yeah?"

“We have a small change in plan; the crystal of air is on an island. We’re going to have to sail there.”

“Oh.”

CHAPTER 16

ENCOUNTER

Before they discussed further about plans to build a raft or even buy a ship they had to go to a market to resupply. They got on the horse and rode across the plains to Nazura market. When they got there, they saw the usual – the traders, the stalls, the tents. But what they didn't expect to see was dozens of soldiers from Chalium, brandishing their swords and grinning mercilessly. They were clearly waiting for them, as they would have heard about the murder of five of their own soldiers and the King of Chalium would have sent more soldiers to deal with them.

Catastrophe and Jess got off their horse, holding their crystals. The soldiers were almost tempting them to attack but there was something else going on. They wouldn't knowingly tempt two people with the power of the elements to attack them.

Catastrophe and Jess nodded and they walked forward unaware that an arrow was pointing at them from a nearby tree. The bow, which was being held by a man watching their every move, twanged and shot the arrow. As the arrow flew through the air, it created a whipping noise. This triggered Catastrophe to look behind him and face the arrow.

He couldn't move quick enough, so he braced himself, pushing Jess out of the way so she wouldn't be in harm's way. He waited for the arrow to hit him but he could feel nothing. As he opened out his arms and lifted up his head he realised that there was a large rock in front of him that clearly wasn't there before. Did the Earth crystal do this? Did it protect him? That question would have to wait as the Chalium soldiers realised that their trick did not work so they charged forward towards Catastrophe and Jess.

Jess threw a fireball which exploded on the floor in front of the soldiers causing them to fly backwards and landing on the dusty soil. Jess didn't kill them so that they could rethink their decision. However, these soldiers were not very clever and did not stop for one moment to realise that this girl could harness the power of fire. They rushed forward, and they were pretty much asking for a beating as Jess scorched them slightly, one by one.

Catastrophe took out the Earth crystal and clenched it, hoping it would do something, and it did; on the grass which the Chalium soldiers, a red and black plant was growing, curling its way through one of the soldier's leg and it seemed to tighten its grip as it grew even taller. It then tightened the grip so much the soldier's right leg went numb and he knelt to the ground, clenching his leg in agony. This same action happened with the other soldiers in a matter of a few seconds.

Catastrophe turned round, got the Water crystal out and clenched it; a burst of water shot out, directing its way towards the sniper with the bow and arrow splashing him and causing him to fall out of the tree. He ran into the market, flailing his arms about as he never wanted to deal with these people ever again.

"Right! That's over." Sighed Jess.

"Yep. All we need to do now is buy a boat."

"Why?"

"Don't you remember? We have to sail to the island which holds the wind crystal!"

"Where could we find a shop that sells a boat here? This is about a hundred miles from the coast."

"Well this market is one of the biggest here so we don't know what we could find. Let's get looking."

CHAPTER 17

SET SAIL

It turned out that Jess was right, there were no boats. This changed the plan even further as they now had to ride to the coast and find materials to build a raft and a sail as the weather wasn't looking too good now. They decided that they should ride to the coast and make camp halfway through the trip as nightfall would be close. They would then ride to the coast at dawn and build the raft at around afternoon. They would be ready to sail in two days.

There was also another problem too. This curse that would be upon Railux Kingdom would have started now right? Or the longer that Catastrophe and Jess would take would determine how bad the curse would be? Anyways they had to ride to the coast now and build a raft quick enough to get to the island so that they could get to Railux castle sooner to end the curse.

"Ready?" Asked Catastrophe, who was quite excited to be sailing a ship after a month.

"Let's go!"

They rode on and on until they were close to the coast. And when they were near the coast, after a day and a half's trip they were relieved. However, there was a lot more work to be to done. They had to build a raft using logs, vines to bind them together and many more things.

"Alright Jess, you get the logs and I'll get the vines and some cloth to make the sails."

"Sounds good."

Jess went in the direction of some palm trees which were on the edge of the beach. The sand was a beautiful shade of gold, the cool water lapped at Jess's feet, fizzing and bubbling. Even though the sun was beating on her back and beaming into her eyes she couldn't help but smile relaxingly as the wind caressed her face. The waves ahead roared and rolled down, crashing onto the shore followed by a soft hiss; peeling away at the sand below her feet. To rest on the beach would be unwise but Jess did so anyway and it felt like a warm hug. Jess, who was quite tired after the long and arduous trip here, stretched out her arms and legs which made her look a bit like a starfish. Jess's grin transformed into a sweet smile as she lied there and never wanted to leave again. This was the life Jess wanted to live; bathing in the sunlight on the beach, swimming in the shallow sea and not doing anything else. Many years ago, Jess thought being the princess of Railux would mean she could do anything, have anything.

However, she was a renowned warrior and she couldn't distract herself with these thoughts nor rest for even a minute as there was work to be done- she ran to the palm trees to make up some lost time and took out her dagger and started chopping down the tree. Every blow seemed to do not much more than the last. Fortunately, she finished in a few minutes and dragged the log over to the other side of the beach where Catastrophe was. It was quite tiring but Jess didn't want to show it. When she got there, Catastrophe asked,

"Hey there, what held you up?"

"Oh, erm…the trees took a long time to cut through," stammered Jess.

"You miss your old life, don't you?" said Catastrophe, who saw Jess when he was coming back with the vines.

"No, I'm perfectly fin…" Jess couldn't lie to him and confessed, "I just wish I wouldn't be a princess sometimes, I wish I could live my life at the beach, doing nothing but admiring the sunshine and feel the cool breeze of wind caressing my face."

"I know how you feel, but remember we're doing this together, and everyone is depending on us to end the curse on Railux Kingdom. Look, I haven't told anyone about this before but you know how there are great stories about me being brave and heroic?"

"Yeah..?"

"All of those stories are accidents-I didn't do those out of bravery, nor did I do those because I was trying to be a hero. They were all accidents. I'm sorry I didn't tell you earlier, I should've said som-" He was interrupted by a short and sharp kiss. Even though it lasted a few seconds, it felt like an hour. They then parted.

"Sorry, I didn't mean to- I was… It's just I think you're perfect as the way you are. You don't need to be heroic. You already are."

"Wow, thanks." Catastrophe was almost speechless but there wasn't anytime to think about it. "Now what do you say we build this raft?"

"Let's do it."

As Jess went back to get more logs, Catastrophe took a moment to realise what had just happened. He then went back to work tying the logs together with the vines he collected. No matter what the weather was like, they had to launch the ship today otherwise there would be more of a delay to getting all the crystals and the curse on Railux Kingdom would get worse.

After a few hours, they collected enough logs and made a raft. Catastrophe and Jess added a sail because there was a high chance of stormy weather and they would definitely need to steer their way towards wind island. The raft was ready.

The storm was nearly here as the great black clouds rumbled ruthlessly, ready to annihilate whatever stood below it. Catastrophe and Jess put in a tremendous amount of effort as they pushed the raft towards the start of the endless ocean. They had to calculate every turn of the sail or they would be dead. This journey was going to be rough. They jumped on the raft, angled the sail and let the unpredictable waves carry them to the island of the Air crystal.

CHAPTER 18

INVASION

Back at Railux castle, King Tyger was in his bedroom, and had his head in his hands as he was getting even more worried about the curse. He knew he could count on his daughter and the great Captain Catastrophe to end it but what if something happened to them? Was he not as caring as he should've been? He realised that he had not been spending enough time with his family and treated her daughter like she was a soldier. She may have not showed it, but Jess wanted to have fun. King Tyger was about to write a letter to her, asking her to return but as he was about to pick up his quill, he noticed that the quill was shaking, and so was the ink pot, and the table. It turned out the whole room was shaking like there was an elephant stampede inside.

King Tyger then heard shouting and panicking outside and was about to put on his kingly outfit until suddenly his advisor bashed through the door and was panting, "Your Majesty... Monster... Outside... Castle... bigger than anything I've seen!" The king rushed outside to the front balcony and could see large groups of people running and screaming. He then looked up and could see something in the distance; a colossal creature heading in their direction. It was as black as night and had a mass purple spikes on its arms, legs and head. Behind it was darkness, like an infinite amount of night and darkness. It was the curse. It was coming.

"Get the people to the caves! And ready the weapon, when my daughter comes back we're going to have to be prepared as that's the only way to destroy it. Right now, all we can do is slow it down. The war is here, Mansley, we have to make decisions that will decide the future of Railux."

"Yes Your Majesty, I'll arrange soldiers to escort the people to the caves. Please be careful sir."

"Don't worry about me Mansley."

Mansley hurried out, leaving King Tyger alone. After all these years, this was it. His father had told him many stories about the curse and seeing it in real life was shocking and unbelievable. He went back into his room and opened a secret floorboard next to the bed. As it creaked open, more screams could be heard from outside the castle. He rummaged around and found what he was looking for- the Ternion. The powerful weapon that was designed to hold all 5 crystals and use them against any opponent. It could only be used one more time. Thousands of years ago, a similar war happened and the previous king consulted wizards and witches all over the world to make the Ternion. They used it and claimed to have destroyed the curse. The Ternion was nearly broken and could only be used one last time before it would be unusable. Clearly, they didn't destroy it fully as it was back so King Tyger had to use it one last time. All that he could do now was wait for Jess and Catastrophe to get here as soon as possible. He wrote a letter, sent his fastest bird- his falcon and watched the bird disappear off into the horizon, heading for Wind Island.

Catastrophe and Jess battled the waves on their raft as they were getting closer to Wind island. Surprisingly, the waves weren't as rough as Catastrophe thought as the logs holding together nicely. It was then at that sudden moment they felt a gust of wind hit them so hard the sail ripped off and slapped him in the face causing him to fall onto the damp logs.

"Oh no! The sail is gone!" Shouted Jess, as he lifted Catastrophe up. However, that was going to be the least of their problems. With no sail, they were heading in a completely different direction and that was not good. If they were heading somewhere other than Wind island, they couldn't even fight whoever had the wind crystal. Suddenly, a massive, cloud-shaped hand swept down from the great black clouds and scooped up the raft; with Catastrophe and Jess on it!

"Woah!" Screamed Jess, trying her best to hold on to the raft. When the raft started shaking violently she slipped off, but was caught by Catastrophe. He hoisted her back up and asked, "It's him isn't it?"

Jess said back, in a confused tone, "I don't know, who?"

Catastrophe had then realised, "Gustion, the wind titan!"

Gustion was the monster who guarded the crystal of Air or used it to become this powerful. He was made entirely of clouds and didn't really have a face as it was just a jumble of clouds. He could create storms, fly with no difficulty and easily take the form of any other clouds in the sky to spy on people who were ying to get at him. However, his special ability was splitting himself into smaller versions of himself so he could take on more than one enemy. He was a force to be reckoned with.

Gustion's hand was still pulling them up and up. They were going to go straight through the clouds at this rate and they did. They were above the clouds and started slowing down.

"Why is it whenever we're introduced to a monster, it's always them making the dramatic entrance and not us?" asked an annoyed a Catastrophe.

"I think we have bigger problems than a dramatic entrance."

"Like what?"

Soon, he saw the humongous wind Titan looming over their minuscule raft which from Gustion's point of view, looked like an ant. Then, he spoke in a deep voice like all the other monsters, "Are you alright? That was quite the storm out there!"

Catastrophe and Jess were so gobsmacked they were speechless.

"Aren't you humans meant to talk or something, aha! I know what you are - special monkeys."

Jess soon had enough courage to speak, "Sorry to disappoint, but we're not special monkeys and we're not going to fall for your 'soft talk' trick. Right Catastrophe?"

"I don't know Jess, he pulled us out of the rough waves that were eventually going to break our raft into chips."

"Exactly!" exclaimed Gustion, a little too loud, "I'm Gustion, the Wind Titan and there's only one thing I want to do."

"What is it?"

"I want to stop the curse of Railux. You see, a long time ago, I was a horrible creature who would kill whoever was in my path until one day, I met a man who was well built and seemed to be wearing a crown. That probably meant he was a king of some place but obviously didn't change my opinion about whether I should've killed him or not. He started talking to me and we talked about many things such as culture and family. It turned out he was an orphan and didn't have a real family and I was in the same situation too as I was by myself. We then became very good friends, I would defend his kingdom and he would protect me from people. When he had a son, he told me that I would be his guardian if something happened to him. And then a month later, we were at war with Chailium."

"Why were you at war with them? I thought they stayed out of our way and we did too."

"Because we were fighting over land - a very simple matter but it soon turned extremely bad. Chailium was holding the king's wife hostage to trade with us. The Queen for the land. However, while we were at Doram Bridge (which was the place where the trade was being made) we didn't notice that about 500 Chailium soldiers were at Railux, and might I remind you; Railux was completely unguarded. It was the oldest trick in the book. As soon as the trade was made that would signal for the soldiers to attack Railux."

"And then what happened? Wasn't the king's son unguarded and left with a maid?" asked Jess.

"Yes, the king knew something wasn't right by the way the Chalium king was smirking once or twice and how he could hear a distant laugh from his soldiers. So he told me to go back to the castle, because I was able to move at high speeds, to make sure if everything was okay. I was quite hesitant because I didn't want to leave the king without any protection as I feared the Chailium King was planning something. I went anyway and when I arrived, Railux was in a state I had never seen it in before. It was war. The castle was just a pile of bricks and bodies mounded into a small hill. It was horrendous. I immediately flew in and swept up the Chailium soldiers I could see. But it was too late, the number of innocent lives lost were uncountable."

As Catastrophe and Jess were listening closely to the huge titan's emotional and shocking words, a deafening screech was heard from miles away. It then was complimented by a deep and dark rumbling that sounded like mountains being crushed.

While Gustion didn't have a face, his silence clearly expressed his shock.

"It is the curse." Gustion murmured, although his loud voice made it seem like he was shouting it.

Jess gasped, "No, we haven't got all 5 crystals of Railux. What are we going to-"

"Quickly! We must travel to Railux! Hold on to your raft." Catastrophe and Jess barely had anytime to think or process what was going on, let alone holding on to the slippery logs of the raft. They grabbed on, and then felt a rush of adrenaline as they jutted forward below the clouds where the storm had cleared. Gustion, who looked like he still remembered exactly where Railux was, flew forward.

Because of the immense speed they were travelling at, the wind was pushing relentlessly against Catastrophe and Jess's faces. But despite this, they saw all the kingdoms and areas where they battled for the crystals- Fire(from the dungeons of Chalium kingdom), Water(from the underwater kingdom Aquarion) and Earth(from the cavern of Nazura). These crystals were earned through their determination to end the Curse of Railux and they were soon going to arrive face to face with whatever the Curse was. This was going to be the last stand against the Curse.

Gustion abruptly spoke to Catastrophe and Jess in a serious tone, "I presume you have the crystals ready? There is no need to question how I know you have obtained three crystals already but you must use the powers you have gained to fight the Curse. I will fight alongside you once I have found the king. There is something in his possession that will destroy this curse forever."

"Alright,' said Catastrophe, not questioning any of the things Gustion had just said, "we're ready."

CHAPTER 19

REUNION

King Tyger was holding the Ternion in his hands. It had been a long time since he had seen it. The base was a tube covered with a layer of obsidian and on top of it was the intricately designed wood taken from the Angelica Tree- the rarest type of tree which is said to have magical properties. The tree can only grow once and once the bark has been separated from the tree, it decomposes in around a week. The only way to stop it from decomposing is to preserve it in liquid diamond. The Angelica wood on the Ternion had five gaps in it for the five crystals of Railux. As he examined this part of the Ternion, King Tyger hoped that his daughter and Catastrophe got the message from his eagle.

As King Tyger saw the chaos happening all over the kingdom, he did notice Mansley directing a band of soldiers to gather people towards the caves. The people were going to be safe in the cave systems that went very deep into the ground. As the Curse got closer, King Tyger noticed that the creature leading the infinite mass of darkness resembled a dragon but with three heads and fiery purple eyes. Normally King Tyger would know his enemy and it's potential but in this case he had nothing to go off except his trust in the mythology and power of the crystals and his daughter with Catastrophe.

Suddenly a sonic boom was heard from the west side of the castle. A large human shaped cloud emerged from the growing dark sky. Although it was difficult to see, you could just make out an abnormally shaped object travelling with the cloud. King Tyger was bewildered; was this part of the curse? And why did he have a feeling he had seen this cloud creature before?

As Gustion emerged into Railux Kingdom, the people of Railux were pointing and staring at the phenomenon. Jess was speechless. She was home, but this was not the home she wanted to come back to. As her eyes were locked onto Railux Kingdom, Catastrophe intervened as he saw the three headed dragon the size of Railux kingdom itself carrying a coal black sky slashed with purple streaks behind it, "Now that… is a great catastrophe."

Gustion, who slowed down and came to a halt over the ocean separating the Curse and Railux Kingdom, said, "Catastrophe, Jess, do you remember the plan?" Catastrophe and Jess nodded in synchronisation. Jess was going to wait on the raft to be taken to the castle where she would hopefully find her father. Catastrophe however was waiting. He didn't seem like he was brave enough to jump. He peered over the edge- it was at least a 100 metre drop. As he was peering over the edge he could have sworn Gustion shook the raft a little because the next thing he knew, he was falling.

Catastrophe pierced the water. While this may have seemed to the people of Railux a confusing plan, they did not realise that the growing mound in the water was a head and soon, shoulders were seen. The power of the water crystal was unmatchable. You see, Catastrophe had become the water giant in Nazura with only a limited supply of water but in the ocean there was virtually no limit. Catastrophe was becoming ten times the size of the water titan he was when he was fighting Grokan. However, Catastrophe stopped growing in size. The water crystal was glowing in a lit and unlit pattern. It didn't matter as the main priority was to get all the people of Railux to safety. That meant he had to fight the thing that got him into this journey for the crystals. The Curse.

CHAPTER 20

BATTLE FOR RAILUX

The Curse was getting closer. It was now about 40 ship-lengths away from Catastrophe. The three headed dragon leading it seemed to be focused on just destroying Railux. Catastrophe advanced, then sped up to a running pace. The dragon started sensing hostility and gave a loud deafening roar in response. The shockwaves from the roar were so strong, it pushed Catastrophe back.

Then the dragon started making sounds. Only that these sounds were getting louder and louder and higher pitched. Catastrophe realised it was charging up for some kind of ranged attack. The dragon's necks all started glowing with purple and at once, it fired three purple lightning bolts at Catastrophe. The attack was instant but the water in his vast body neutralised the attack. Catastrophe had to be smart about this. It was definite that if he got too close to the Curse, it could have devastating effects on him. He decided ranged attacks were the way to fight back.

Catastrophe clenched his crystal and saw two pillars of water rise up. The pillars of water directed towards the dragon's chest(which was only about 20 ship-lengths away) and blasted off like a bullet, impaling the dragons crystal-armoured chest. He repeated this with eight pillars of water. Little by little, the water jets eroded bits off the crystal armour. Catastrophe felt the crystal pulse. That must have meant the crystal needed to regain its strength. The dragon, having taken a beating, was vengeful for destruction.

Jess, who landed at Railux, was searching for her father. She was desperate to find him and ignored the deafening battle going on in the background. Gustion flew up and circled round the castle until Jess called out when she spotted a shiny dot on a balcony. As Gustion took her closer to the dot, she realised that it was a reflection from the crown on her father's head. King Tyger was astonished. His daughter was on a raft that was being held up by a titan made of clouds. Despite this occurrence, Jess was unable to express how happy she was. She jumped off the raft and leaped into her father's open arms and did not let go for a long time.

"Jessica", said King Tyger, "I am so sorry for not giving you enough freedom in your own life."

Jess, who was trying her best not to cry, eventually gave in. She whispered back, "You don"t have to be sorry for anything Father."

Gustion, who didn't show much emotion, interrupted the conversation, "Apologies if I have intervened but Jess, we must go. Catastrophe is on his own."

Jess, who didn't want to leave her father unprotected, hesitated until King Tyger said, "Jess, go. The people of Railux are depending on you and Catastrophe. Also, you must remember to hold back the Curse until all the people have been evacuated to the caves. Once you have done that, return immediately back to the castle. I believe I have found a way to destroy the Curse but you have to remember that all the crystals should be present. Please be careful Jessica. Now Go!"

Jess, knowing they had only three crystals, didn't have time to say anything back. Gustion had pulled her back on the raft. Jess had a responsibility as the princess of Railux to protect Railux's people.

Gustion spoke to Jess, " I will hold you steady in the air so you have a clear view for ranged attacks. The Curse is extremely dangerous and we don't know how it affects you or me."

Jess nodded in response and as they got closer to the Curse, they could feel the atmosphere change from a chaotic atmosphere to one of pure terror and destruction. Catastrophe, who was dodging the dragon's oncoming ranged attacks would not be able to hold his ground for that long. He then heard a 'Woosh' from behind him. The dragon noticed something as well. As it was charging up for its second attack(this time, a different sequence of sounds were heard which resembled a rumbling of a volcano about to erupt.), Catastrophe, who felt that he still was drained of energy, felt quite helpless in the situation. The three heads of the dragon then unleashed a huge roar together followed by flaming rocks and boulders infested with purple crystals released from its dark opening between its jaws. Those rocks and boulders were heading straight for Railux. Catastrophe couldn't possibly get there in time to stop the boulders from hitting the towns and villages.

Something strange happened, as the boulders were arcing towards Railux, they burst in a combination of purple crystals, rock and fire. Jess was here!

"Catastrophe, we need to keep the Curse as far away from Railux as possible!"

"I did kind of realise but how much time do we have?" bellowed Catastrophe, who felt a rush of energy from the Water crystal.

"10 minutes! They're getting the last few people evacuated!"

Ten minutes was a long time to keep the Curse at bay. And considering it was only focused on destroying Railux, it would keep moving. It looked like the Curse was going to reach Railux in five minutes.

Catastrophe then responded, "I'll have to get closer to it! Jess and Gustion, stop all the ranged attacks that will hit Railux!"

"Understood." Said Gustion. Gustion positioned himself above Railux where Jess would lay the counter attack if any boulders came their way.

Catastrophe advanced forward, charging towards the dragon. Catastrophe brought a fist up and just as one of the dragon heads was about to strike Catastrophe, it was pounded by a 50 tonne force of a punch just under its chin. The dragon screamed in response and as Catastrophe was ready to punch again, he didn't notice the long tail with a cluster of sharp purple crystals coming around at high speeds. The tail whipped him hard in the head causing Catastrophe to lose balance and fall.

However, as the tail was whipping, it released some large crystals that were the size of the stalagmites in Aquarion. These crystals were very sharp and streamlined, so they were travelling relatively fast. Jess was ready though, as the crystals got closer she shot multiple fireballs at each one. However, the crystals were not affected by the fire at all. They were heading for the village, there was nothing they could do.

Jess screamed, "NO!" Until she realised that in the village, huge stones grew out of the ground where the crystals would hit and smash into pieces and they did that. The crystals simply disintegrated when their sharp point made contact with the thick rocks.

Catastrophe, having noticed what had happened after he fell, immediately took out the crystal of Earth, it was glowing green! The Earth crystal had bonded with Catastrophe so well that it could almost predict Catastrophe's thoughts. This gave Catastrophe an idea.

Catastrophe retreated and noticed that he was ever so close to Railux kingdom. The Curse was getting dangerously close. However, the last few people were making their way into the caves. Catastrophe clenched the Earth crystal and watched as the dragon came to a halt. It's legs were unable to move. The reason it was unable to move was because the Earth crystal made building-sized coral rise up from the shallow part of the ocean and latched on to the legs of the Curse as it waded through the water. The dragon clearly wasn't happy about it as it roared with a high pitch. Jess, who noticed the people had been evacuated to the caves, alerted Gustion. Gustion flew towards Catastrophe, who was coming towards them. As Gustion slowed down in front of Catastrophe's massive head made of water, Jess said, "Catastrophe we have to get back to my father! He says he knows how to destroy the Curse! And quickly as well! The dragon won't be held up forever!"

"Got it!" responded Catastrophe, he clenched his Water crystal and felt himself getting closer to the ocean. Gustion flew down and caught Catastrophe in the air.

They were making their way to the castle where King Tyger was, frantically waving his arms. Gustion flew down to the balcony he was on. King Tyger spoke,

"Jess, Catastrophe, give me your crystals." Catastrophe took the Water crystal and the Earth crystal out of his pocket and gave it to King Tyger. Jess took the Fire crystal out of her pocket and handed it over too.

"Where are the other crystals!?" asked King Tyger, "where is the fifth crystal? The power will be unbalanced without them!" As he said this, he heard a cracking sound from where the dragon was standing. The coral was breaking. The dragon was going to crush Railux in the next few minutes.

'The power will be unbalanced without them' Catastrophe said to himself. It made sense! Catastrophe shouted, "Gustion take me down to that village! There is something there I need to get!" Gustion could sense the seriousness in his voice and did not hesitate to take him to the village. When Catastrophe landed there, he soon found what he was looking for; a fragment of one of the purple crystal spikes shot by the dragon. He picked it up and Gustion took him back to where Jess and King Tyger were.

King Tyger took out the Ternion, and put the three crystals in three slots of the Angelica Wood. Catastrophe put the fragment of the crystal spike in a slot. Catastrophe said, "Just trust me on this." There was no time to argue anyway.

The dragon was starting to walk on the coast of the kingdom, with the cloud of darkness closely following from behind. King Tyger then exclaimed, "Where is the crystal of Air!?"

Gustion said, "My time has come. Your Majesty, you may have never seen me in your life, but I knew your father for decades. He asked me to promise, just after you entered the world, to keep you safe from harm's way. Every day, I have been watching the kingdom, ensuring that nothing would hurt you. I couldn't protect the old king of Railux but I am determined to protect this one." Ignoring King Tyger's astonishment he said, "There is no time. I am the crystal of Air. It powers me. My sole purpose was to stop the Curse of Railux and that is what I intend to do right now."

"Gustion No!" exclaimed Catastrophe. But it was too late, Gustion was shrinking, metre by metre until he turned into a tiny, opal-coloured crystal. Catastrophe, knowing that Gustion wouldn't want him to waste time, picked the crystal up and pushed it in the Ternion's last slot. The dragon was now crushing the villages it was walking on, determined to get to the castle. It's eyes were flaming with anger. Then, the dragon stopped. It's three heads were acting differently, almost as if it was scared.

Then a flash of light came from the Ternion. King Tyger, Jess and Catastrophe were all holding it. Then, streaks of light(red, blue, green, white and purple) emerged from the

Ternion and like a lightning bolt, struck the dragon in the chest where it had the most crystal armour. The dragon roared in pain. The light started acting differently now. It sent streaks of light towards the dragon, but this time it was covering it like a net of light. It engulfed the dragon completely and then once it looked like the dragon was covered from head to tail in light, it started decaying. It was shrinking at such a rate that if you blinked you would miss half of the action.

Catastrophe was silent, mesmerised in the moment as well as Jess and King Tyger who were blinded by the light from the Ternion. The dragon was now unrecognisable to what it was a few moments ago. The cloud of darkness was disappearing. The light of the normal world was returning. The Ternion looked like it was going to crack into pieces from the sheer power of the five crystals. Then, after what felt like hours, a great BOOM! occurred and one final flash of light sent a huge shockwave that flung Catastrophe, Jess and King Tyger back.

CHAPTER 21

DAYLIGHT

Dazed, Catastrophe got up and pulled Jess up. King Tyger got up while also noticing that the Angelica wood on theTernion was cracking. Catastrophe and Jess turned around as they heard a soft fizzing sound from the wood. It was decomposing. The diamond coating on the wood didn't do anything to slow the decomposition of the wood. Catastrophe and Jess were quite astonished and tired, so tired that they simply were physically not able to speak. The wood was getting smaller and smaller until the four crystals of Railux and the fragment of the Curse's dark crystal fell out into the palms of King Tyger's hands. All that was left was the polished obsidian coating around a tube.

When Catastrophe had enough energy to speak, he said, "So, we did it?"

Jess, who felt relieved, said, "Yes, Catastrophe, we did it."

King Tyger however, was ecstatic, "The Curse is no more! The kingdom of Railux is safe. I shall send for Mansley to alert the other soldiers." King Tyger ran back into the castle, leaving Catastrophe and Jess alone.

Catastrophe noticed that in King Tyger's excitement, he placed the crystals on the floor. Catastrophe picked all four crystals and then it was at that moment he realised that the fragment of the crystal spike from the Curse had disappeared. He soon realised that the other fragments of the dark purple crystals that were previously littered across the coast and the villages were gone too. The balance in power had shifted as the Curse was destroyed. This must have meant that any remaining parts of the Curse couldn't exist. This is why there was such little evidence of the Curse and why only stories could be told about it's existence.

Jess leaned over and looked at the crystals Catastrophe was holding. Fire, Water, Earth and Air. The four elements that provide balance to the world. Jess took the Fire crystal and noticed that the crystal did not glow anymore. Catastrophe could notice this as well with the other three crystals he was holding.

Catastrophe turned to Jess, "Do you think we should keep them?"

Jess, who expected this question, answered, "I have been thinking about this. Our purpose was to find the crystals of Railux so we could end the Curse. While doing so, we made a few enemies along the way. Who knows, maybe every creature and human in this world could be looking for these. I'm not sure if we have just endangered the life of every person living in Railux or - " Jess stopped midway her sentence as she looked back at her palms. The Fire crystal was gone. She looked under her feet and couldn't see anything.

"The Fire crystal, where is it?" frantically asked Jess.

"It was in your hand a minute ago!"

As Catastrophe was looking for the crystal he saw flashes of fire. Then, flames curled and weaved their way upwards to form a flame shaped like a woman. Jess, who immediately noticed this, stumbled backwards and gasped.

"Please calm down." Said the flaming figure, "I do not want to harm you." Catastrophe's breathing slowed down and didn't realise that Jess was clinging on to him. When Jess came to her senses, she let go almost immediately.

"I am Inferna, mistress of Fire, I have been watching you on this journey ever since you released me from the body of Morphon."

Catastrophe, who pieced the information together, was about to speak but was cut off by Inferna, who knew exactly what Catastrophe was going to say next.

"Yes, I am the Fire crystal. There are others like me which you have bonded with as well." As Inferna said this, a puddle of water swivelled up to look like a human-sized version of Catastrophe when he was made of water when fighting against Grokan.

Another figure grew from a tiny leaf into vines that formed the legs, torso, arms and head of a human but made with a combination of leaves, flowers, vines and branches.

Finally, the air in front of Catastrophe and Jess turned foggy and clouded their vision. As Catastrophe was clearing the fog he noticed a familiar figure.

Inferna then said, "We used to have a long history with your kingdom, we were quite well known thousands of years ago.

This is the master of water; Aguano," She gestured towards the figure of water. Aguano nodded towards Catastrophe. Catastrophe nodded back.

"This is the master of Earth; Eredo." Eredo was the human-shaped figure made of possibly every kind of plant and vine. He was quiet, most likely studying Catastrophe's facial expressions.

"And you have already met the master of Air, Gustion."

Jess, shocked and relieved with joy at the same time, asked, "Gustion? We thought you were gone."

Gustion couldn't show any facial expressions but he did have some emotion in what he had to say, "I have never gone through the process of returning to my crystal form. That is why you have always seen me as my original form as a figure and also why I believed I wouldn't return back when I transformed into the crystal of Air."

Inferna then spoke in an assertive manner, "We all used to coexist with the humans and creatures not only in this kingdom but elsewhere around the world. We had unlimited, raw power at our disposal but it was important that we controlled such power and ensure that we did not disrupt the process of evolution of all beings in this world. One being however, did not understand the need to control such power. He believed that all the masters of elements should rule this planet with brute force."

"What was his name?" Asked Catastrophe, who was intrigued by the story so far.

"Dakar, master of Darkness. The 'Curse' you just destroyed was his doing." Inferna continued, "I disagreed with Dakar's immoral plan along with many other masters of elements but some agreed with him either as a result of fear of being punished if they did not agree to support Dakar or because they selfishly saw benefits for themselves if Dakar was able to overrule the opposing masters."

Jess then asked, "How did we find your crystal forms scattered across random locations? Why were you only visible when we slew creatures?"

Aguano was now speaking, his voice sounding like someone with water in their mouth, "We believed with the powers we had, we could stop Dakar from continuing with his insane plans to rule the world. However, Dakar had overpowered us. He could perform feats of magic that cannot even be performed by the vast majority of masters. He banished us to many locations across the world.

To make sure we would not return to stop him from carrying out his plans, he trapped us within the souls of inanimate or animate things. I was banished to the Kingdom of Aewaledora where I was trapped in a trident that had the power to transfer me to William Neptune's son. Then I was extracted from his son and transferred to Krolion, the beast which lived in the deep caverns under Aquarion. When Krolion was destroyed, I could not be transferred to anything so I was left as my original crystal form; the crystal of Water."

"Thank you Aguano," said Inferna, "But Dakar did not only banish us, he crippled us, making us almost useless-"

Catastrophe interrupted, "How do you make sure that the inhabitants of our world are not destroyed? If your elements don't exist then surely we should be dead?"

"You are correct. Dakar, if he had the chance, would be most willing to destroy us. But elements cannot be destroyed because they are needed to maintain balance in the world. Also, Dakar would ideally rule the planet like a god. He would want all beings to worship him as their supreme leader. Therefore the worst damage that can be done to us is banishing us from the Realm Of The Elements(which is our home) and crippling us so that our own powers cannot be used for any other purpose except maintaining balance in the world. This way, we couldn't escape the things that trapped us inside for centuries."

Now, coming on to you," said Inferna directly speaking towards Catastrophe and Jess, "You may have many questions but as I speak, Dakar grows stronger and he will have known that something has happened with the Curse that he set upon you."

Catastrophe and Jess understood by nodding. Inferna continued, "We have been with you throughout your journey to end this 'Curse' that was upon your kingdom. But we knew from decades ago that this 'Curse' was coming. We made a decision thinking that the myths that have been spread about the crystals of Railux could mean that someone would try and find the four crystals of Railux to free us of the things we were trapped inside."

"But why did you not find the other masters by yourselves when we freed you?" asked a puzzled Jess to Inferna, who was the first crystal form Catastrophe and Jess found.

"Because we needed a host. I shall explain further; when we were extracted from whatever was housing our crystal form inside them, it's almost like being recreated. We were almost powerless and weak because of Dakar's actions. A worthy host who could control our very limited power to help those in need will prove a resourceful and strong-willed host."

"So, you gave us the abilities to defeat those monsters? Because you needed a host to give you strength to reignite your abilities and powers?" asked Jess.

"Well, in a simple way of understanding it, yes." Said Inferna, who was glad that Catastrophe and Jess were understanding her.

Inferna then said, "We would like to thank you for releasing us from the things we were trapped in. We are ever so grateful for the bravery and the sacrifices you made to save us. However, Dakar knows that we have escaped and he will come for us. He will try and destroy everything in his path to achieve rule over this world. We do not wish for your kingdom or your people to come to harm so with great regret we will have to leave."

Aguano cut in, "Whenever you need our help, we will be there."

"Really?" asked Jess.

Gustion said "Yes, think of it as repaying our debt for freeing us."

Jess laughed and said, "Thank you."

Aguano said, "Farewell Catastrophe, farewell Jessica." and faded away. Eredo nodded and shrunk until he was a tiny leaf, also disappearing at the end. Gustion, who lent out a cotton-like arm, tried to shake Catastrophe's hand. Catastrophe awkwardly put his hand where he thought Gustion's hand might be and pretended to shake his hand. His hand got cold and wet quite quickly. Gustion soon faded away leaving a cloud of mist.

Inferna, who was the last to leave, said, "It has been a privilege to know you and if we do not see each other again, know that we will remember and honour you. Farewell." Inferna's exit was the most dramatic, vanishing in a flash of flames.

"So I assume that answers the question of whether we are going to keep the crystals or not?" Catastrophe asked.

"Yes, it does."

After a long pause, Catastrophe then asked Jess something he wanted to ask for a while, "What did you think of me when I told you that everything I did was an accident, that everything I did wasn't a result of me trying to be heroic?"

Jess moved closer to Catastrophe and placed her hand on his shoulder, "I believed that you weren't a great fighter when I first saw you. In fact, I didn't want you to come with me on this journey of finding the crystals of Railux when I met you."

Catastrophe was surprised at this brutal honesty, and Jess could notice this. She laughed in response and then continued, "But as I saw you fight, and saw your determination to be a better person, I saw the qualities of a hero, the qualities of a person who is not for himself, but for the greater good."

Catastrophe was shocked that he wasn't a clumsy, confused person who didn't know his potential but a person who had stepped in the shallow waters of his potential and was beginning to discover who he really was.

Jess moved even closer to Catastrophe, now leaning against him with her arms wrapped around him. As Jess observed the sunlight reflecting of the waves just off the coast of Railux Kingdom, she said, "It's beautiful isn't it?"

"Yes, yes it is."

Vaibhav Neela is the author of '*Captain Catastrophe's Great Catastrophe!*'. With over two years of experience of writing stories and conducting creative writing workshops in schools, Vaibhav has a unique ability to write stories that take the readers to another world of imagination. Vaibhav also received a Silver Arts Award for '*Captain Catastrophe's Great Catastrophe!*' in 2021 and has encouraged many children to write stories.

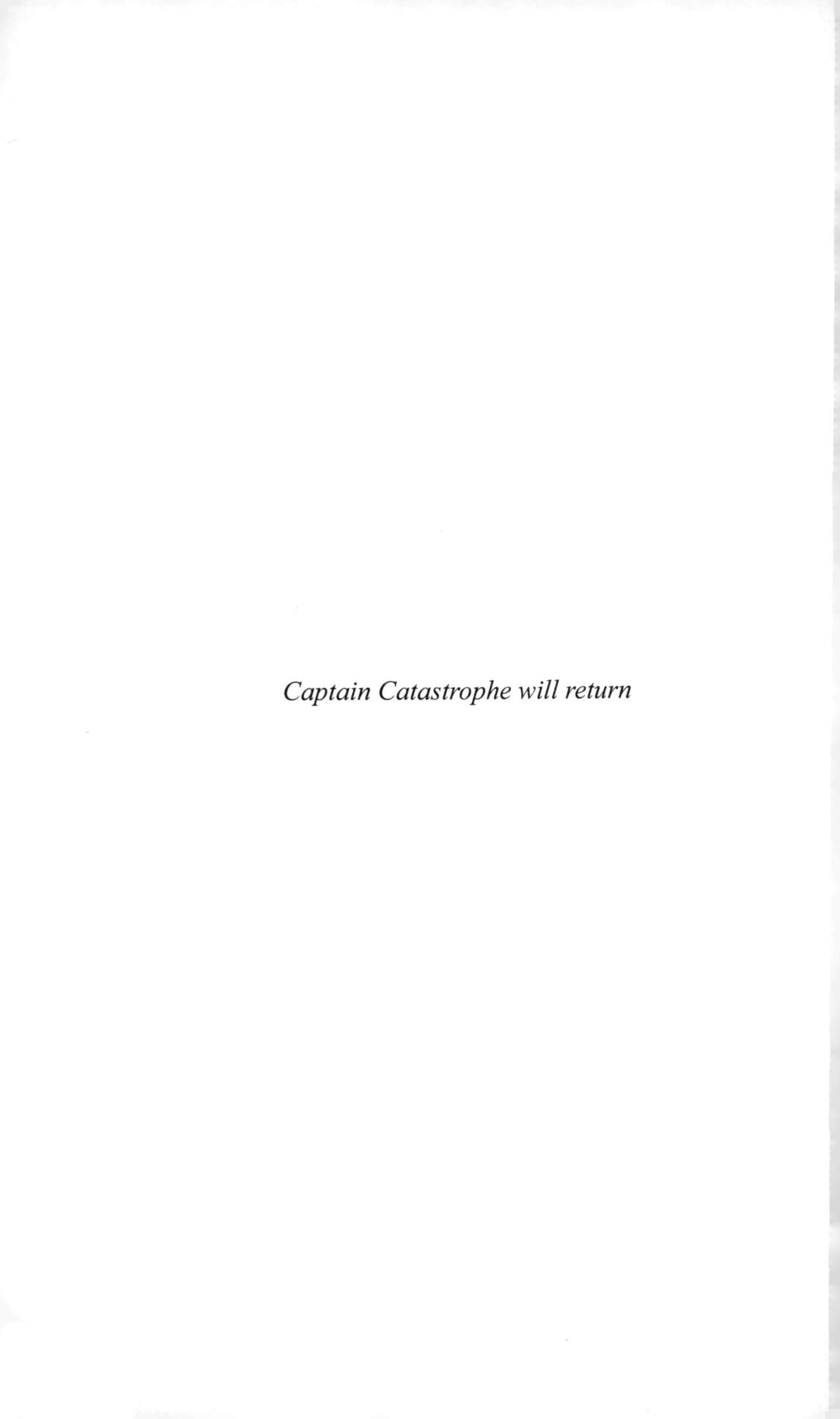

Captain Catastrophe will return

Printed in Great Britain
by Amazon